Praise for
The Kingdom Series

"The Kingdom Series is what every Christian boy dreams of—a King Arthur story with a lesson and without Merlin! These books are an excellent choice for any family."
—GLEN, age 13

"My son is truly a picky reader, and he's already read these books five times!"
—V. H.

"Right from the start, I was wrapped up in the stories and couldn't put these books down. It showed me how to be filled with compassion and love for others. The Prince rules forever!"
—JUSTIN

"I was entertained, intrigued, and very blessed with Chuck's allegories. He brings truth to life from the Scriptures regarding the spiritual conflict God's people are engaged in and can expect to be in the future, culminating in the final and glorious victory we are waiting for. The reader is treated to an anointed and fresh insight into the greatest battle of all ages as he or she is drawn into a medieval setting with noble warriors and devious villains. The result is great reading enjoyment and enlightenment for the soul!"
—TERRY, age 52

Look for other books in the Kingdom Series:

THE KINGDOM SERIES

BOOK 4

KINGDOM'S CALL

CHUCK BLACK

MULTNOMAH
BOOKS

KINGDOM'S CALL
PUBLISHED BY MULTNOMAH BOOKS
12265 Oracle Boulevard, Suite 200
Colorado Springs, Colorado 80921

Scripture quotations and paraphrases are taken from the New King James
Version®. Copyright © 1982 by Thomas Nelson Inc. Used by permission.
All rights reserved.

The characters and events in this book are fictional, and any resemblance to
actual persons or events is coincidental.

ISBN: 978-1-59052-750-4

Published in association with The Steve Laube Agency, LLC,
5501 North Seventh Avenue, #502, Phoenix, AZ 85013

Published in the United States by WaterBrook Multnomah, an imprint of the
Crown Publishing Group, a division of Random House Inc., New York.

MULTNOMAH and its mountain colophon are trademarks of Random House Inc.

Library of Congress Cataloging-in-Publication Data
Black, Chuck.
    Kingdom's call / Chuck Black. — 1st ed.
        p. cm. — (The kingdom series; bk. 4)
    ISBN: 978-1-59052-750-4
    I. Title.
PS3602.L264K555 2007
813'.6—dc22

                                                    2006101825

Printed in the United States of America
2012

10 9 8 7

To the men that mentored, counseled,
encouraged, and prayed for me.
Thank you, my brothers!

CONTENTS

HERALD OF THE PRINCE

 I am one who is compelled to share a tale with you for the express purpose of keeping its truth alive. My name is Cedric, from the city of Chessington.

I am a Knight of the Prince in the kingdom of Arrethtrae, and however grand that might sound, were you acquainted with me, you would know that my failings are equal to my victories. On my own, I am no more than a pauper. It is the Prince for whom I live and for whom I fight. He raised me from the mire and made me a son. I will aspire to serve Him to the utmost, and perhaps my duty to Him will be fulfilled more as a herald than as a warrior, for if my quill and ink capture your attention and cause you to ponder the chronicles of this great kingdom and the story of the Prince, then I am content.

I am one in a long line of gallant knights. We await the orders of the Prince, for He has brought us to this point in time to deliver the people of Arrethtrae from the treachery of the Dark Knight. The darkness of Lucius's evil army is descending on Chessington, but the might and wisdom of the Prince will triumph. Our waiting here reminds me of the waiting years before the Prince returned for His people.

After the Prince left to cross the Great Sea, our numbers greatly increased, despite tremendous ridicule and persecution. I have known many brave Knights of the Prince throughout the kingdom, and the tales of their great deeds are grand indeed. However, of all the gallant knights I have encountered and fought beside, there is one whose flame for the Prince seemed to burn brighter and hotter than any other. I think this is so perhaps because he first wielded his sword as a dreaded enemy of the Prince. It is the transformation of the hearts of men like him that anchors the truth of the Prince in my own heart. The impact of his quest to bring the cause of the Prince to the kingdom is deniable by no one!

The story of this gallant knight is one that inspires all Followers of the Prince…and possibly even those who are not. There is not much time, for Lucius and his Shadow Warriors are near, but come with me for a moment back to the waiting years to hear the story of one of the greatest knights of Arrethtrae. As with all worthy stories, it is one that begins with the Prince. 🔲

CHAPTER ONE

A NOBLE CAUSE

Gavin saw the blade of his foe flash toward his chest and brought his own sword to bear the powerful blow just in time. His adversary pressed hard with a volley of powerful cuts that would have placed any excellent swordsman into a defensive retreat, but Gavin stood strong and did not yield his ground, for he knew that Chessington's only protection from Outdwellers like these thieves and marauders lay solely in the powerful swords of the Noble Knights. Gavin was in the midst of a hundred flashing swords, and the sound of battle was in the air all around him. It was once again a battle to defend the precious treasures of Chessington and her people from the chaos of a kingdom filled with repressive and greedy brutes.

Although Gavin was a young knight, he had acquired the skill of an expert swordsman. He did not hesitate or retreat from his enemy's onslaught, but masterfully met each blow with the mighty sword he wielded, using quick and powerful combinations that nearly found their mark. Feeling the hesitation in the fight of his enemy, he replied with another slice and a quick thrust that put his opponent down.

"Behind you, Gavin!" came a shout from a fellow Noble Knight.

Gavin turned to engage his new adversary, but it was too late. A sword blasted into his helmet and sent him reeling to the ground facedown, dizzy and in pain. He rolled onto his back and realized that his helmet had been knocked clean off of his head. The world was a blur as he tried to focus and regain control of his senses. His new opponent wasted no time in bringing a deadly vertical cut down on him, and Gavin felt helpless, for it was impossible for him to bring his own sword into a protective position in the split second that remained. As his opponent's weapon raced toward his chest, Gavin heard the yell of a familiar voice and a powerful sword came across to meet the one that was about to end Gavin's life. As the two swords collided, Gavin rolled and recovered to see a fellow knight engage and attack his would-be executioner. Within a moment, the foe was bleeding and retreating from the fight. The knight turned and looked at Gavin with concern.

"Are you all right, Sir Gavin?" he asked.

"I am now. Thank you, Lord Kifus. You have saved my life once again!"

The two men positioned themselves side by side, looking for the next fight, but the marauders were under retreat. The two forces slowly disengaged, and the sounds of clashing swords diminished.

Gavin turned to face Kifus and took a deep breath in an attempt to recover from the intensity of the fight. He offered his hand in appreciation. Kifus removed his helmet and smiled at Gavin.

"You are welcome. I should expect you to return the favor someday," Kifus replied as he took Gavin's hand.

Kifus had personally mentored Gavin, who had served as Kifus's squire for many years until he earned the right to become a knight himself. Gavin's skill with the sword and his zeal for the Code won him that right earlier than any other man in the history of the Noble Knights. Now, at twenty years old, he had already become one of the top five knights in Chessington, carrying on the tradition of his family. In reality, Gavin's skill had the potential to transcend that of every Noble Knight. In the heat of a sword fight, he felt as though he could predict the moves of his opponent. He did not have to contemplate his next maneuver; it seemed to be a natural ability that flowed through the muscles of his arms and legs. An older knight's experience occasionally led to his defeat, but it was only a matter of time before the rising young knight would be second to none, not even Kifus.

The Noble Knights gathered around Kifus and rejoiced in their victory.

"For King and Code!" Kifus exclaimed.

"For King and Code!" echoed the force of Noble Knights.

They were powerful, well-trained knights, and the citizens

of Chessington were thankful for their protection. Through the years, they had defended the borders of the city against every kind of enemy the kingdom threw at them, and there were many. Without a wall to protect it, the city was vulnerable, and the Noble Knights knew it was their duty to protect every Chessington citizen. These were the King's chosen people, and the Noble Knights were the chosen of the chosen. Anyone not a citizen of Chessington was considered an Outdweller, and although not all were enemies, the distinction was clearly evident in their dealings with such people.

Even within Chessington, some of the Noble Knights became arrogant in their position of prestige, but not Gavin. He was a man who was zealous for the cause of the King and desired to live by the letter of the Code with perfection. Although he harbored no ill feelings toward Outdwellers who were not enemies, he knew that he was Code- and honor-bound to the citizens of Chessington exclusively.

"You fought well today," Kifus said to Gavin as they rode their mounts into the city. Many people had lined the streets to cheer their champions, and most of the knights basked in the adoration.

"Thank you. Your training of the knights has proven to be our salvation once again," Gavin said.

Kifus appeared indifferent to the compliment.

"My younger sister has asked of you, Gavin. I think a visit from you would be well received."

Gavin became slightly embarrassed. Leisel was a beautiful girl, and he felt honored that Kifus would consider him an appropriate suitor for his sister, but he did not expect such an offer. Gavin was a serious young man and felt that the time and energy it would take to cultivate a relationship with a woman would take away from his duties as a Noble Knight, especially in times like these, when all the kingdom seemed bent on destroying their beloved city.

More cheers rose up from the streets as the Noble Knights turned a corner, and the powerful steeds they rode raised their heads to look even more noble.

"I am honored, Lord Kifus. Perhaps in a few days there will be an opportunity to afford a visit. Thank you."

Kifus nodded and smiled. "I shall inform Leisel."

The knights gathered in Kifus's courtyard to hear his final words, for evening was fast approaching and the weariness of battle was closing on them.

It was the privilege of the leader of the Noble Knights to reside in the remnants of the grand palace built by the people for Lord Quinn many years ago. Although it was but an echo of its former glory, the palace was still the pride of Chessington. The great hall of the palace was where the Noble Knights often met to discuss the affairs of the city. Kifus conducted frequent training with the knights in the front courtyard. Although the palace was the usual domain for the knights, contests between the knights were always held in the city square nearby. This was to allow the citizens an opportunity to witness the skill of each of the Noble Knights as they fought to determine their ranking within the order. The people of Chessington loved to attend the duels, for it comforted them in these days of turmoil.

Within the palace were many halls, rooms, and chambers that were once used for various functions, but most were now empty and unused. With the exception of Kifus's sleeping quarters, which were in a separate building near the center of the palace grounds, the Noble Knights were granted full access to the palace.

"Well done, fellow knights," Kifus said, still atop his mount. "You have upheld the Code and protected the King's city once again. You fought well, and I am proud to be the leader of this noble force. We shall meet in the great hall in one week at the usual time."

Kifus drew his sword and held it high. "For King and Code!"

The knights all drew their swords. "For King and Code!" they replied in unison. The men then disbanded and returned to their homes.

Gavin lingered within the courtyard until he was its sole occupant. He dismounted and tied his horse near the edge of the courtyard.

"Well done today, Triumph." He stroked the beautiful white coat of his stallion. Triumph nickered and seemed to nod his head.

Gavin walked to the steps of the great hall and entered. He continued to a door at the back of the hall, the sound of his boots echoing on the stone floor in the silence of the large empty room. The door's massive hinges and lock were indicative of the treasure that lay behind it. Gavin reached beneath his armor and produced a key that symbolized years of disciplined training, for only Lord Kifus and the top five knights were given such a key. As a young squire in training, he had purposed in his heart to attain the elite position of one of those five, but it was not for self-glory. It was for moments like this...freedom to access the contents of this room whenever he desired.

The lock clicked loudly, and Gavin pulled on the thick doors to open them. They creaked in resistance but gave way. He lifted an oil lamp beside the doors before entering, then walked down a narrow hall and into the inner chamber. The lamp flooded the small dark chamber with light to reveal the treasure within. There was no gold, silver, or any precious stones—those were in a lesser chamber and were not the treasure that Gavin desired to see. Within the room was a lone table that held the precious treasure. Gavin placed the lamp on the table, and its light revealed an ornate wooden frame that held a single piece of parchment.

He drew his sword and placed it before him as he knelt before the

Articles of the Code. Written in the hand of the King Himself, Gavin felt that he was in His presence here. Gavin's heart seemed to draw strength from being so near to the Code. There was not a doubt in any corner of his mind as to his purpose in the kingdom. It was to honor the King and to live by the Code.

"In the presence of the Code, I once again swear my allegiance to the King," Gavin said quietly. "For truth, for justice, for honor…I offer my life to the service of the King and will defend His city and the citizens thereof."

It was Gavin's heart to see the King face-to-face one day and not be ashamed of his duty as a Noble Knight. He knew the King was more noble, more mighty, and more just than any man of Arrethtrae could ever be. He also knew that only the King was worthy of such devotion, and so it was to the King alone that Gavin pledged his allegiance. The Chamber of the Code was a place Gavin frequented often, for it affirmed in his heart this allegiance. His visits to this chamber usually followed a battle or a time of adversity. And although other laws had been enacted by which the people lived, only the Code contained the mark of the King. Very few people had actually seen the Code, for the Noble Knights considered it a privilege reserved for nobility.

After a few moments, Gavin exited and locked the chamber. He mounted Triumph and began the journey home. As he rode, Gavin's thoughts turned to the battle of that day and to the offer Kifus had made regarding his sister. Some of the men seemed so at ease and natural when courting a lady, but such was not the case with Gavin. He felt as though he would rather fight an enemy than face the awkward conversation that awaited him. And yet, he could not deny the fact that he was intrigued by her interest. He wondered if he was going to spend the next few days as distracted as he was right now.

Fortunately—or unfortunately—an incident occurred that would change everything.

CHAPTER TWO

TREACHERY!

It was awkward to say the least. The Noble Knights were all gathered in Lord Kifus's great hall two days after the "incident," and there was no boisterous bragging or jesting, only whispers. This day it was the incident that brought the powerful knights together, but the reason for the gathering also made it awkward. Sir Gavin knew that even two days was too long to wait for a discussion of the incident with Lord Kifus and the other knights, but he also knew that Lord Kifus needed time to recover from the sting of embarrassment.

Lord Kifus was the last to enter the hall, and when he did, all the knights rose to their feet in respect. As Kifus arrived behind his seat at the head table, the room resounded with the bright noise of steel on steel as all one hundred Noble Knights drew their swords and raised them above their heads.

"For King and Code!" they shouted in unison.

Kifus returned his sword to his scabbard, as did the other knights. Soon all the men were seated, and the awkward silence returned.

Lord Kifus seemed different today. As the leader of the Noble Knights, his authority was unquestioned. Over the years, he had proven himself the most skilled warrior in all of Chessington. No one had ever dared to challenge Lord Kifus—until the incident. He was a powerful knight who possessed not only skill with the sword but also a sharp and cunning mind. His dark hair and beard were slightly streaked with wisps of white that added to his noble stature. As he gazed across the room, most of the knights averted their eyes to avoid his stare. Gavin wanted to as well, but his curiosity about how Lord Kifus would handle himself overpowered him. For the first time in his life, Gavin saw a crack in Kifus's confidence. It was not easily seen, for it was covered with anger and spite, but it was there nonetheless.

The incident of two days ago hadn't left Gavin's mind for even a moment. He had been there, and a stranger had embarrassed not only Lord Kifus but every Noble Knight in the square. Quite simply, a girl had been caught stealing, and the law called for Lord Kifus to cut off her right hand as punishment. It was a harsh retribution, but it was necessary according to the law of the Noble Knights. Without order, chaos would reign. It was then that this stranger intervened and challenged Kifus and two other knights. He looked like a peasant until he drew a magnificent sword and prevented the young lass from enduring the edge of Kifus's sword.

Kifus naturally turned his sword upon the stranger, and soon it was evident that this impetuous man was much more than a brave-hearted, foolish peasant. The duel between the mighty Lord Kifus and this stranger was brief and decisive. The man actually disarmed Kifus and then countered the attack of two other Noble Knights simultaneously. Gavin could not deny the mastery of this newcomer, but his words of treachery against the Noble Knights, the King, and Arrethtrae enraged him.

Kifus straightened his back and spoke. "Undoubtedly there has been much private talk about what happened the other day. The whispers of the city are an insult to the Code, to the King, and to all of us Noble Knights."

Kifus stood, and deep anger reddened his face as he leaned forward to finish his words. "Do not let your own lips be guilty of this insult!"

After a moment of silently staring at the knights, he seated himself and regained his composure.

"Gentlemen, we have a problem. There is a skilled man of defiance among us. What say you on this matter?"

Sir Jayden rose to speak. He was a fierce man, quick to action and patient with none. He was one of the two knights who had attacked the stranger from behind. "This traitor to the King deserves one thing and one thing only—death! No one has the right to defy the authority of the Noble Knights or to say such treasonous words against the King and live!"

"Hear! Hear!" Many knights exclaimed their approval.

Sir Camden rose and settled the hall with outstretched

arms. He was one of the wise knights. Everyone knew that his actions were carefully planned and well thought out.

"Sir Camden," Kifus addressed him. "Impart some wisdom to this assembly."

"Lord Kifus," Camden began, "despite his apparent skill with the sword, this stranger most certainly is a traitor. However, even a man of skill can be a fool. And if not a fool, then most certainly a lunatic." Sir Camden paused to let his fellow knights think on his words.

"Perhaps he is both," Camden continued, "for only a lunatic would claim to be the Son of the King while dressed in peasant garb, and only a fool could find followers more foolish than himself to join his cause, as was evidenced in the square two days ago."

Many nods of affirmation came from the other knights. "What does one do with a fool and a lunatic, Sir Camden?" Lord Kifus asked.

"In time, his followers will see their folly and the false hope of personal grandeur, and the city will see his lunacy. Time, Lord Kifus. Time will kill this stranger for us." Sir Camden seated himself and basked in his own words of wisdom and the accolades from surrounding comrades.

The assembly continued, with as many opinions expressed as there were knights present. Gavin listened to them all and was disturbed. During the incident, he had watched not only the stranger but also the response of the people. They seemed to be taken with this man despite his treachery, and Gavin knew how potentially dangerous that was.

At one point the hall was filled with the noise of dozens of simultaneous discussions among the knights. Gavin kept silent and did not freely offer his thoughts to the others.

Lord Kifus watched the men, and Gavin watched Kifus. For the first time since he had known Kifus, it was apparent that he was uncertain of what to do.

"Sir Gavin!" Kifus shouted above the rumble of discussions. The knights quieted and turned their attention to Kifus and Gavin. "We have not heard your thoughts on this matter. How should the stranger be dealt with?"

The gaze of the entire assembly fell on Gavin. Though young, he was a powerful knight, and his skill with the sword had won him the respect of every man present. He had taken fourth place in the training competition in the square two days ago. Gavin knew his height was less than that of the average knight, but his build made up for it. With loosely curled black hair, he didn't feel particularly striking—except for his penetrating blue eyes which showed a deeply felt charisma that he believed shone through. He was a man of unwavering convictions and was grateful for the trust of the other knights, who recognized his devotion to the Code.

Gavin chose his words carefully as he stood to speak. "Lord Kifus and fellow Noble Knights, through our bodies flows the blood of nobility, for we have been chosen by the King to defend this kingdom and His Code. My blood boils with anger at the insolence of this stranger in attacking what we know is true and right. However, it is not our emotions that must govern our actions. I agree with Sir Camden, for the people appeared to be enamored with this man's traitorous but persuasive words of false justice. However, I too am confident that the effects of his deceit upon the citizens will be brief. Therefore, let us be patient and let his own foolishness reveal itself to the people. He must be punished—that is certain. Let us not forget the offenses, but mete out justice at a time when the people will not despise *us* for it, but rather *him*."

After some time of reflection, Lord Kifus stood. "Well spoken, Sir Gavin. We will wait—but we will also watch. Sir Demus and Sir Braden, follow this man and learn all you can of him."

The two knights nodded.

Kifus raised his sword. "For King and Code!"

"For King and Code!" echoed back the sound of ninety-nine powerful knights—knights who would never forget the incident.

CHAPTER THREE

A PEASANT'S THREAT

 The days following the meeting of the Noble Knights were, for the most part, uneventful. As the weeks passed, Sir Demus and Sir Braden gathered as much information about this stranger as they could. They spoke to people who'd had encounters with him and had listened to his words when the stranger spoke openly in the square about the King and the kingdom.

For some time there was little to report, and the months passed without serious incident. But eventually it became apparent to Gavin that the stranger's influence over the citizens of Chessington was growing stronger.

Lord Kifus called for another meeting of the Noble Knights. They gathered from all across the city of Chessington into the great hall. As usual, there were many pockets of discussion throughout the room. Gavin looked toward Demus and Braden. They had chosen a table off to the side of the hall and were not joining in the discussion. Oddly, they were not even speaking to each other. Gavin supposed they were gathering their thoughts for the report they were to give the assembly.

The hall was called to order, and Lord Kifus rose with an air of authority. As time had separated him from his encounter with the stranger, Kifus had slowly reclaimed his pride and prestige among the men.

"Sir Demus and Sir Braden, tell us what you have learned of this traitor."

Gavin noted that Kifus's selection of Demus and Braden as observers had not been an impromptu decision. Kifus's actions, Gavin knew, were always purposeful and planned. Of all the Noble Knights, Demus and Braden had the best rapport with the people. They were good friends and were often seen in Chessington together. Kifus knew the people would be much freer with information about the stranger to Demus and Braden than to any of the other knights.

Of the two men, Demus was the more reflective and Braden the more outspoken. Braden rose to offer their report. "Lord Kifus and Noble Knights of Chessington," Braden spoke loud enough for all to hear. "We have followed this stranger and observed his actions for many days now. We can confirm that he is indeed a traitor, for he is actively training a force of men in defiance of our law. He is continuing his heresy of speaking against us and of proclaiming himself Son of the King."

"This is an outrage!" Sir Jayden rose to his feet with a clenched fist and a red face that clearly indicated his anger. "Lord Kifus, how can we let this continue? We are being shamed and disgraced before our own people, and we sit and do nothing!"

The assembly of knights joined with Sir Jayden in denouncing the stranger and his actions. There were many calls for death to the stranger. The roar of protests filled the hall, and Kifus found it difficult to regain order.

Kifus eventually quelled the knights. "Sir Demus, what have you to report?"

Demus looked a bit surprised. He slowly rose, and Gavin noticed that Demus and Braden momentarily locked eyes.

"Lord Kifus, what Sir Braden reports is indeed true. However, action must be taken with great caution, for this stranger has an ally that we do not—and a powerful one it is." Demus paused and looked as if he did not want to continue.

"Who is this ally you speak of, Sir Demus?" Kifus asked.

Demus spoke hesitantly, for this statement would offend most of the knights present. "The people of Chessington." Numerous looks of disdain were directed at Demus.

Kifus looked concerned.

Demus continued before losing the men's attention. "We have won the respect of our citizens, but we have not won their favor. This stranger has done both. His words and his skill with the sword have captured the hearts of the people in a way I have never seen. Whatever action we take must be done without stirring the people against us. His influence is growing more and more each day, and time is not on our side."

Demus sat down, as did Braden. Kifus looked long and hard at Demus, and the knights waited for a response.

Kifus led the Noble Knights because of his skill with the sword, but a savvy mind was as much a weapon for him as a sharp blade. "Sir Demus speaks truth to us, gentlemen." He nodded toward Demus. The tension in the hall abated somewhat, and Gavin saw Demus relax slightly.

"The stranger is not only skilled with the sword but is a cunning deceiver as well. We all know the foolishness of the people. This man has taken advantage of this and has become a great threat to the Code, the King, and our beloved city." He looked toward Braden and Demus. "Is the stranger ever alone?"

"Not that we have ever seen or are aware of," Braden replied. "He often trains with his men in the hills east of Chessington."

"Very well," Kifus said. "We will move when he is in the hills, away from the people. We know his men are unskilled and foolhardy. They are not a threat. Braden, Demus, and Jayden will attack him and reveal him to be what he truly is—a traitor." Kifus looked to the three men. "Upon his defeat, you will command him to leave our city forever. But if he resists unto death…then so be it."

This plan pleased the men, and Jayden looked delighted at the prospect of killing the stranger. The assembly was dismissed, but Gavin remained longer than usual. He walked toward Braden and Demus and heard quiet but strong words being exchanged between them. At Gavin's approach Braden saluted and dismissed himself.

"Sir Demus, your services to the King have been admirable," Gavin said.

Demus bowed his head slightly. "Thank you, Sir Gavin."

Demus and Gavin were fair acquaintances, and there was a genuine mutual respect between them. Gavin quickly scanned the room and relaxed his tone to one of familiarity. "You have never hidden your heart very well, my friend. What troubles you?"

Sir Demus was one of the older Noble Knights, and the slight wisps of gray near his temples seemed to add to the wisdom that was always present in his words. He never rushed into a situation without first considering the consequences and evaluating every option.

Demus looked into Gavin's eyes as if to question his motives. "I do not want to fight this stranger," he said plainly.

Demus was a quiet man, but Gavin had never known him to be fearful. Or worse—a coward.

"I can understand your reservation, Demus. He is a skilled swordsman. There is no doubt of that. But surely with three of you the fight cannot last long and you are sure to be victorious."

"I am not concerned with the outcome, Gavin," Demus said. "I am concerned with"—Demus looked at Gavin directly—"our cause."

Demus had just revealed a very dangerous possibility to him. Gavin paused and tried to discern the sincerity of Demus's comment. "What are you saying, Demus?" Gavin could feel anger rising within him. "That this stranger is something other than a traitor? That there is some flaw in our judgment of this madman?"

"No, of course not," Demus said with some reserve.

Gavin looked sternly at Demus. "You have a duty and an

obligation to fulfill your mission. Do not let the charisma of a lunatic cloud your judgment, Demus!"

Demus's countenance revealed his own anger. "Are you questioning my loyalty, Gavin? I have dedicated my life to defending this city and my brothers here. My sword will not fail to defend the honor of the Noble Knights!"

Demus turned abruptly and left Gavin without another word. Gavin was further disturbed and somewhat surprised, for such a response from Demus was uncharacteristic. The influence of the stranger was reaching far beyond a few disgruntled peasants in the city, and Gavin was quickly becoming aware of the magnitude of the danger. He hoped that this surprise attack by three of their best knights would end it all, but in the shadows of his heart he saw a beginning—not an end.

CHAPTER FOUR

TROUBLED HEART

 Demus, Braden, and Jayden converged upon the stranger without regard for the four peasants who were with him. The peasants were no match for the Noble Knights, and everyone in the hills that day knew it. Just prior to their engagement, one of the peasants threw his sword to the stranger. Wielding a sword in each hand seemed as natural for him as handling just one. The knights tried to encircle him, but steep terrain prevented their attempt, so they maneuvered apart to divide the stranger's attention.

Sir Jayden aggressively attacked from the left and Sir Braden from the right, while Sir Demus engaged the man from the front. Seeing the stranger's mastery over Kifus was incredible, but experiencing it firsthand was nothing less than terrifying for Demus. Within a few blows, Demus was awestruck at the power and skill of this traitor. With a sword in each strong hand, he thwarted and countered the flashing steel of three swords simultaneously. It seemed as though the stranger knew the exact position and direction of each attacking sword even with his eyes averted. With each cut, Demus's sword did not simply meet resistance; it met immovable force equal to that of a brick wall. There was no giving or fainting of strength.

It was Jayden who made the first reckless attempt to kill the stranger. Apparently perceiving an opening, Jayden thrust at the stranger from the left. In one quick motion, the stranger parried the thrust to his back, blocked a cut from Demus's blade, and slammed the pommel of his sword into Jayden's head. Jayden fell immediately to the ground, unconscious.

Demus and Braden intensified their fight, for the error of their misjudgment was overtaking them. Demus countered a cut and brought a vertical blow from above upon the stranger. Braden timed a knee-high cut from the side, attempting to bracket the stranger between the two approaching blades with no escape. But to Demus's surprise, the stranger brought both swords up to block the cut from above, seeming to leave himself open to Braden's deadly cut from below. In an instant, the stranger leapt above the approaching cut and brought a forceful heel into Braden's chest, which sent him reeling to the ground without any air in his lungs.

Demus now faced the fierceness of the stranger's fight alone, and fear overwhelmed him. It was no contest, and Demus knew that he was only one or two blows shy of death.

This stranger, a true master of the sword, wielded two swords that had no equal. Demus held his sword before him and retreated one step, hoping only that his end would be quick and merciful. The stranger spun each sword in a circular motion and brought such strength to the double crosscut on Demus's blade that his sword was sheared in two.

Demus prepared for death as he looked into the stranger's face. In battle, the gaze of the victor over his defeated adversary was always full of wrath, for the blood of aggression required it. But as Demus looked into the stranger's eyes for the first time, he was dumbfounded. There was no wrath—no fierce anger. Demus's fear left him, and he wondered at his own heart. The stranger's gaze penetrated him like the steel of a blade but left no wound.

By now Braden had recovered and was approaching them from behind. The stranger placed a sword at Demus's neck, but Demus was no longer afraid. He knew his life belonged to this man, and he did not resist.

"Drop your sword," the stranger said at Braden's approach.

Moments later, Demus and Braden, carrying Jayden between them, were walking away from the stranger. Demus paused and turned to look at the stranger once again. They had come to kill this man, and he spared their lives.

"Are you truly the King's Son?" The question left Demus's lips, and he felt as though someone else had spoken it. The question was spontaneous, something he could not contain.

The stranger's eyes pierced Demus. "What does your heart tell you?"

♛ ♛ ♛

Beyond the hill, the three men approached their horses, and Jayden began to stir. Demus and Braden laid him on the ground to give him a chance to recover before the ride back to Chessington. They remained silent. Questions and excuses filled their minds until they heard the approach of a rider. Sir Gavin galloped around the hill, dismounted, and quickly came to Jayden, who was now holding his head and moaning. Gavin knelt beside him.

"What happened? Is he all right?" Gavin quickly searched Jayden over for any fatal wounds.

"He is fine," Braden replied tersely.

Gavin rose and faced Demus and Braden. "Is the traitor defeated?"

Demus and Braden looked at each other and waited for the other to speak. Their silence was enough, and Gavin felt the anger rise within him again—anger that they had failed, anger that this traitor was still standing in defiance of the Noble Knights. It was an emotion he was not accustomed to, but it was present and building. Gavin looked toward the hill where the three knights had come from and began to draw his sword.

Demus grabbed his arm. He looked Gavin squarely in the eye. "He has the power to kill you in an instant!"

Gavin quelled his anger, seeing truth in Demus's concerned expression. He relaxed and let his sword completely return to its scabbard.

"Sir Jayden needs attention, and Kifus will want a full report," Gavin said. A more severe course of action was required, much more severe!

It was a silent ride back to the great hall of the Noble Knights, and Gavin did not envy the position his comrades were in. Once again, the stranger had shamed the best of the Noble Knights, and his influence over the people was growing, not diminishing. What troubled Gavin most, however, was the change he sensed in Demus. Was it possible that the stranger's influence was reaching even into the realm of the Noble Knights? Gavin resolved in his mind to arrange a private conversation with Lord Kifus.

Demus, Braden, and Jayden met with Lord Kifus at the palace that evening, and Gavin accompanied them. In a chamber off the great hall, Gavin remained silent as the three knights described the encounter with the stranger. Kifus listened intently but did not show any disdain for their efforts or their defeat, as Gavin had expected.

When they had finished, Kifus stroked his beard and turned away from the men.

After a moment of silence, Braden voiced the question Gavin was thinking as well. "Where could a man with such skill come from?"

"The skill of this traitor is even greater than I thought," Kifus responded. "It is a skill beyond the capabilities of mere men; there is no denying this. Since his words are blasphemous against the Code and the King's Noble Knights, there is only one answer as to the question of his origin." Kifus turned to face the men again. "He comes from the domain of the Dark Knight!"

Gavin could feel the alarm and fear among his comrades as they considered this possibility. To his knowledge, no one had ever seen the Dark Knight, and Gavin often wondered if the legend of his might was more myth than truth.

"Is such a thing possible, Lord Kifus?" Gavin asked.

"It would be unusual but very possible. A man under the influence and training of the Dark Knight would be a formidable foe. We must use every weapon at our disposal and be more cunning than the Dark Knight himself if we are to overcome and destroy this powerful enemy of the King."

Gavin looked toward Demus, but there was almost no expression on his face.

"Gentlemen, we must act quickly and decisively. Remain here while I send for some of the other knights to devise a plan," Kifus said.

Before long, another thirteen of the top Noble Knights had arrived. Kifus ordered his servants to bring refreshments to the knights as they assembled in the great hall. A young servant boy quickly set about filling the knights' goblets with fresh wine. Gavin refused his portion, for he wanted to think clearly. He noticed that Demus had refused as well.

"Noble Knights, it is clear that time has not resolved our problem as we had hoped," Kifus said seriously, with an edge of frustration.

"The imposter in our midst is gaining more influence with each passing week. His insults toward the Noble Knights are becoming more brazen, and his followers are growing in number. This man is an ally of the Dark Knight and an enemy of the King. We must act now if this threat to the Code and the kingdom is going to be eliminated!"

The knights joined in Kifus's enthusiastic denouncing of the stranger, and Jayden in particular seemed satisfied at last with the course they were taking. Gavin looked once again at Demus and saw anguish in his countenance; he had suspected that there was conflict within Demus's heart. Gavin had intended to bring his concern about Demus before Kifus in private, but he saw in the next instant that perhaps that would not be necessary.

Demus rose from his seat. "Lord Kifus, I have heard this man's insults toward the Noble Knights, but I have also watched his actions. I find it difficult to believe that he is of the Dark Knight and his domain."

The silence that followed was thick. Kifus looked toward Demus, and Gavin could see anger in his eyes. Much to Gavin's surprise, Demus did not shrink back but continued with his bold words.

"I must insist that the council of these Noble Knights reconsider any action that would take the life of this man, for I have not yet seen or heard of him breaking any article of the Code!"

Jayden walked toward Demus as though he were ready to strike down a traitor. "Sir Demus, your words hint of treason. You must be mad to defend this traitor!"

"Demus is granted the right of opinion just as any other

knight here, Jayden," Kifus said. "I suggest you consider your words carefully, Sir Demus, for this assembly will deliver justice to the stranger, and that justice will come by the noose of a rope—with or without your consent."

All eyes fell upon Demus. Gavin had never felt such tension in the hall of the Noble Knights before. Demus boldly took in the stares of his fellow knights until at last his gaze came to Gavin. Gavin slowly shook his head in a final attempt to warn his friend against foolish action.

Demus stood and faced the knights. "Then let it be known that I do not consent, and I will have no part of this plot!" He turned and exited the hall.

Gavin was sad and angry at the same time. He knew that any friendship he had with Demus was over, and he pitied Demus's foolishness. But Gavin's anger with the stranger was now rooted even deeper in his heart. He felt a fire in his bosom that he knew would only be quenched when the stranger was gone…or dead.

"You can see the extent of this traitor's influence," Kifus said, attempting to regain the attention of the knights. "We must act decisively and with full force."

"The stranger's skill with the sword is overwhelming," one knight said. "How do we take a man who has no weakness?"

Kifus thought for a moment. "The traitor does have one weakness," he said. "His followers! He may be able to defend himself against great odds, but he cannot defend all of his inept followers. We will attack them, and he will then yield to us."

Numerous discussions between knights revealed unanimous approval for Kifus's plan. He was a brilliant tactician, and that had never been more obvious than now.

"How will we know when and where to attack his followers?" one knight asked Kifus.

Kifus smiled wryly. "There is one amongst the followers who has a fancy for silver. Prepare yourselves and the rest of the men. When I call, be ready to ride, for we will end this man's treachery once and for all!"

Kifus dismissed the knights but asked Gavin to remain. "Gavin, these are becoming desperate days, and I am concerned with the loyalty of some of the knights. I need men I can trust implicitly."

Gavin looked directly into Kifus's eyes. "There is no breach in my resolve to defend the Code and the order of the Noble Knights against such imposters as this stranger. You can trust me, Lord Kifus. I give you my word."

Kifus smiled and placed a hand on Gavin's shoulder. "I believe you, Gavin. And in the days to come I will need to rely upon you heavily, for all that we believe in and live for is at stake."

"By the sword of the King I swear my allegiance to Him and to the Code. This stranger and his followers must be eliminated!" Gavin said.

Kifus nodded and Gavin turned to leave. After he had walked a few paces toward the door, Kifus called to him.

"Gavin, the work we must do will become, shall we say, a bit *messy.*"

Gavin looked at Kifus, confused by the remark.

Kifus continued, "There are certain aspects of this job that are best suited for men like Sir Jayden and Sir Bremrick. You needn't involve yourself too deeply in the method of this justice. Do you understand?"

Bremrick was as brash a man as Jayden but much more distasteful in his habits. Gavin tried to have little to do with him. Gavin did not know how to respond to Kifus, for he did not fully grasp what Kifus was trying to say.

Kifus looked squarely at Gavin. "You have great influence among the other men and I need your leadership, but I want you to keep your distance from this…this imposter who claims to be the King's Son. With regard to him, your role will be one of observation only."

"Lord Kifus, I am fully capable of dealing with the insolence of this imposter. Believe me, neither my resolve nor my stomach will become weak," Gavin said.

"I do not question your resolve or your stomach, but I am not asking; I am commanding. There is no need to bloody your hands with this affair. I need your influence among the men, but you will observe from a distance."

"Yes sir," Gavin replied.

Kifus nodded and Gavin departed. On his way through the city, he felt compelled to stop and talk with Demus at his home. He did not understand the heart of his former friend, and he hoped that a few words of reason would bring him back to his senses.

The two men stood in the foyer of Demus's beautiful home.

"How have you been so fooled by this man, Demus?" Gavin asked.

"You have not felt the power of his sword or looked into his eyes as I have. His words are not the words of a lunatic—or an imposter," Demus replied.

"I do not want to look into the eyes of a man under the influence of the Dark Knight and be lured by his words of deception as you have."

"He could have easily killed me today," Demus said. "And the moment I looked into his eyes I saw more nobility and compassion than I have ever seen in anyone else. How is that the evil of the Dark Knight? No, he is not an evil man. Instead of taking my life, he spared it. We went to kill him, and yet he showed us mercy. That is true nobility, Gavin, not treachery!"

Gavin looked on Demus sadly. "You have been bewitched, my friend, and it will cost you everything." His eyes shifted to take in the riches of Demus's home.

"To take up my sword against this man would cost me the very character of my heart, and I am not willing to pay that price!"

Gavin shook his head as he left Demus's home. The influence of this stranger was far-reaching indeed, and he wondered for a moment if Kifus was worried that he too could be swayed by his cunning words. Gavin steeled himself for the great task ahead, for he felt in his heart that a day of judgment would bring deliverance for the people of Chessington...even if they didn't yet realize they needed it.

CHAPTER FIVE

THE SILENCE OF A STRANGER

The Noble Knights rose up for battle on a blistering hot day. With the exception of two or three, all were mounted and riding into the country east of Chessington. The earth shook as the hooves of nearly a hundred battle horses thundered across the grassy fields. Triumph seemed as agitated as Gavin, and for the first time he found it difficult to control the beast.

Gavin's armor felt heavy today as he wondered if the followers of the stranger would fight. The knights wanted only one man, and the thought of killing fellow citizens of Chessington to get to him was contrary to his own character, even if they were mere peasants. Though not worried about the outcome if such a fight were to occur, Gavin could not have been more anxious than if they were riding to meet five hundred savage warriors.

He was also concerned with how the rest of the people of

Chessington would react to them seizing this stranger. The stranger had won the hearts of many people.

Gavin saw Kifus confidently leading their mighty force and was thankful for his wisdom and his ability to control the people. Beside him rode a man Gavin had never seen before.

As they approached the base of the hill, Kifus halted the men and spoke briefly with the accompanying rider. Gavin watched as Kifus handed a small pouch to the man, who then galloped speedily back toward Chessington.

Kifus spoke only loud enough for the knights to hear.

"The traitor and his men are a short distance over this hill. We will split into four contingents and surround them. Jayden, Gavin, and Braden will each lead a contingent. We attack together on my command. For King and Code!"

"For King and Code!" the men intoned and then separated.

Within a short time, Gavin and his knights crested the hill and were charging in unison with the other three contingents. They descended from the hills upon the stranger and his men. Their swords were all drawn, and the sound of nearly one hundred skilled knights thundering toward their enemy on massive steeds was enough to unnerve any man.

Kifus halted the knights as the four contingents joined to form an impenetrable circle around the stranger and his men.

Although the followers of the stranger looked like frightened, cornered rats, the stranger did not. There was a moment of intense silence. Then Kifus moved his steed forward a few paces.

"Today your lies and blasphemies end," Kifus declared.

"Your death and the deaths of your petty servants will restore order to this kingdom once and for all!"

The stranger walked toward Kifus with his sword still sheathed. He stopped midway. "Kifus, your grievance is with me, not my men. Spare the needless spilling of blood, and let my men leave peacefully. I will go with you as your captive."

Gavin looked at Kifus. This was exactly what Kifus had been hoping for, Gavin knew. He desired to one day be as wise.

Kifus hesitated, pretending to consider the stranger's proposal. He did so with an air of authority.

"So let it be," Kifus said. "Make way!"

The mounted Noble Knights opened their ranks and allowed the followers to flee to the surrounding hills unharmed. Once they were clear, the circle of Noble Knights closed in on the stranger until he drew his sword.

What a fool, Gavin thought. *Does he really think he can defeat a hundred mounted Noble Knights?* Gavin glanced toward Kifus and was amazed to see fear on his face. Kifus and the knights paused, but instead of fighting, the stranger threw his sword high above and beyond the ring of knights and surrendered unarmed.

The knights bound the stranger's hands tightly behind him. They proceeded back to Chessington, and Gavin noted that Kifus chose the longest and most public route to the great hall. It was an opportunity to show the people of Chessington that the Noble Knights were truly the supreme authority, despite the turmoil this stranger had caused over the past months. Word spread quickly through the city, and soon the streets were lined with people. The reaction from the onlookers varied from dismay to delight. They followed behind the knights and their captive until they reached the palace grounds. The throng of people grew to such a mass in the outer courtyard that Kifus had to assign extra guards to keep order.

In the great hall, the stranger was placed before Lord Kifus's table. All of the knights gathered to see how the stranger would endure the shrewd words of Kifus. Gavin remained behind the other knights, just as Kifus had ordered. He was surprised when he saw Demus quietly enter the hall and stand across the room, apparently unnoticed by everyone there.

Kifus brought the assembly to order before addressing the stranger. "As Noble Knights, we are the keepers of the Code and the protectors of Chessington. We were chosen by the King to defend justice and honor here among the people. Your acts of treason against the Code and the city of Chessington demand severe punishment."

Kifus glared at the stranger. Gavin had never seen him so intent in his dialogue before.

Kifus took a deep breath and seemed to relax slightly. "However, we will consider a lesser punishment if you will refute all of your preposterous claims."

The stranger did not respond. He only stared at the ground before him. Gavin thought he looked completely defeated, as though he were a helpless lamb. *How did this simple man gain such influence over the people?* he wondered.

Kifus seemed irritated by the silence of the stranger. Without some response or rebuttal, it would be difficult to charge the man. Kifus continued to question the stranger, and his patience seemed to be wearing thin. The rest of the knights were becoming angry as well. After a long and unfruitful interrogation, Sir Bremrick went to the stranger, grabbed his chin, and lifted his head into the air.

"Well, he appears to still be alive," Bremrick stated cynically, and the hall roared with laughter. He then walked past the stranger, lowered his shoulder, and slammed into him, sending the stranger reeling backward onto a chair and then to the floor. More laughter followed, and a couple of the knights brusquely set him on his feet again.

The questioning continued and was met with more silence. Exasperated, Kifus walked around the table to stand directly in front of the stranger. "We heard you claim to be the Son of the King. Are you?"

The room fell silent, and for the first time since the questioning had begun, the stranger lifted his head to stare directly into Kifus's eyes. In that moment, Gavin was shocked at the authority that seemed to emanate from this stranger.

"I AM!" the stranger said. "And there is no man in Arrethtrae who has ever truly fulfilled the Articles of the Code, nor will there ever be. I have come to fulfill the Code so that all men may become true Knights of the King by Me. No one may come to My Father except through Me!"

Shouts of protest from the Noble Knights rose up throughout the hall. The very core of their existence was to live by the

King's Code, and for this peasant to claim royalty equal with the King was blasphemy. Jayden drew his sword and struck the stranger's head with the pommel. The stranger fell to the ground, and blood flowed freely onto the stone floor beneath him. Others descended on the fallen man and began to kick him. The gauntlets they wore struck his back until he was bruised and bleeding everywhere. Kifus did nothing to stop the men, but looked upon the abuse and appeared justified.

Gavin felt the heat of the stranger's insult as well, but he was glad it was the fists of others that brought silence once again to this man. Gavin looked for Demus, but he was gone. When the anger of the knights had abated, Kifus ordered that the stranger stand before him to receive his sentence.

"For the words and acts of treason against the King and the Code, I hereby sentence you to death by hanging."

Shouts of approval rose up from the knights. Gavin looked over the shoulders of his cheering comrades to see the stranger's reaction. He offered none.

CHAPTER SIX

CURSE OF A CHARLATAN

 The following day, word spread throughout the city that the imposter was to be hanged in the city square on the afternoon of the next day. Kifus wanted all the citizens of Chessington to see the judgment of this man. It would serve to show the people that the authority of the Noble Knights was still supreme, and it would eliminate any foolish attempts by his followers to continue in their unsanctioned training.

Over the course of that day, Gavin had many long conversations with other knights regarding the stranger and the remarkable influence he had gained over the people in such a short time. By midafternoon, he was weary of such talk and sought solace in a garden on the palace grounds.

Questions entered his mind that would not go away, and the peace he was searching for evaded him. *Is the death of this man the only way to end the rebellion that is sure to come if we let him continue?* he wondered. *How truly dangerous is this man?*

Gavin's thoughts turned to Demus and the two or three other knights who had disagreed with their judgment regarding the stranger. For just a moment, Gavin entertained a possibility that he had never dared let his mind consider: what if the Noble Knights were wrong? Gavin could only know one heart for sure, and that was his own. He knew that he was wholly committed to the King and the Code, and this imposter had threatened and ridiculed the Noble Knights in front of the entire city of Chessington. That was enough to solidify in his mind that their course of action was indeed the right one, and he vowed never again to question their resolve as a force of nobility to protect the King, the Code, and the people, even against one as skilled with the sword as this imposter was.

"Sir Gavin," a sweet and gentle voice called from behind him.

Gavin turned to see the lovely form of Leisel approaching with all the grace of a princess. He stood to greet her. "Good afternoon, maid Leisel."

"May I join you for a moment?"

"Certainly, my lady. I would be honored." Gavin bowed slightly.

"You seem a bit troubled," Leisel said. "Is there anything I can do for you?"

Leisel came close to Gavin, and they sat down on a stone bench. Gavin had not noticed the beautiful flowers surrounding him until now. Leisel's perfume mingled with the fragrance of the flowers, diverting his thoughts from the concerns of the day. He had taken the opportunity to visit Leisel on occasion over the past few months, but was reluctant to actively pursue a courtship. It was no fault of Leisel's, for she was a beautiful girl and had provided Gavin ample opportunity to advance their relationship. However, with each passing week, he had become preoccupied with the growing threat of the stranger and his followers. As one of the top Noble Knights, his duties were extensive and, at times, overwhelming.

"The city is full of tension, and we have come to an hour of great turmoil," Gavin said.

Leisel looked into his eyes. "Is it true that some of the knights are against the execution of this imposter?"

Gavin hesitated. "They are few, but yes, it is true." Speaking these words made their dilemma feel all the more real. He was also surprised at how quickly Leisel was able to make him feel as though he could spill his whole heart to her. He wondered if this was true for all men and the ladies they conferred with. He was not used to being vulnerable.

"Is this what troubles you, Gavin?"

"Yes. I am disturbed that these men could be swayed by

such an imposter as this stranger. I have fought beside them, and they have proven themselves to be men of courage and valor. And yet they stand opposed to your brother and the rest of the Noble Knights. How is this possible? How could they be so beguiled?"

Gavin looked at Leisel, not really expecting an answer, but he was thankful for the attentive ears of one who was removed from the influence of the politics that often entangled the Noble Knights.

"I do not know, but this I do know: you have a heart that is strong in the Code, Gavin. Your integrity as a Noble Knight will guide our people through this time of deception. Tomorrow all will be set right."

Gavin looked into Leisel's eyes and smiled. "Yes, tomorrow all will be set right." Her words were soothing to him, and he realized what a comfort she was to him during these difficult times. He resolved in his mind to make her a larger part of his life.

Their conversation turned to lighter subjects, and by the end of the afternoon, Gavin had nearly forgotten the troubles of the city…at least for a few hours.

By early afternoon of the following day, the Noble Knights had assembled in the palace courtyard with their prisoner, who was bound and bleeding from fresh wounds. Bremrick was his gruff escort and did not refrain from harsh treatment. Gavin had learned that one of Bremrick's personal servants had joined the followers of the stranger months earlier, and Bremrick's bitterness was evident.

Most of the knights rode ahead and entered the city square to bring order to the throng of citizens that was gathering. Kifus led the remaining fifteen knights, with the prisoner walking in tow behind Bremrick's horse. Gavin chose to trail the procession. When they arrived at the square, it looked to Gavin as though the entire city was present. Kifus made one complete circuit about the square so everyone could see that the imposter was not so mighty anymore. Their final destination was the large oak tree in the center of the square, where the advance contingent of knights had prepared a rope.

The prisoner was set atop a horse, and the noose was placed around his neck. Gavin was amazed at his composure—he did not plead, nor did he look afraid.

Kifus spoke loudly for all to hear. "People of Chessington, this man is guilty of treason against the King, against the Code, and against you. He has lied to you and misled you. He brings chaos to the kingdom. Today justice is served!"

Kifus raised his hand to slap the horse on which the prisoner sat. Strangely, Gavin cringed inside. In that instant he felt as though the entire kingdom of Arrethtrae would split in two. In the depths of his soul, he knew something profoundly significant was happening, and it frightened him. Kifus slapped the horse and the man hung. Triumph whinnied and snorted, and Gavin had to work hard to restrain the steed. Gavin chose to watch the reaction of the people rather than the man at the tree. Some of the people were cheering, and some were weeping.

Gavin recovered himself. *Now it is over,* he thought, for he could not imagine any reasonable person continuing to follow this man beyond his death. After some time had passed and the death of the stranger was sure, it did not appear to Gavin that there was threat of an uprising, so he eased away from the square and the mass of people as quickly as possible. He rode back to the palace, entered the courtyard, and dismounted. Gavin didn't really know how to feel about what had just happened, but he was becoming angry—angry for the months of turmoil this charlatan had caused the people of Chessington. Regardless of today's judgment, Gavin felt that the reputation of the Noble Knights had been tarnished. It was an unpleasant but necessary execution for the preservation and restoration of all they knew to be true.

Gavin walked into the great hall and back to the doors that led to the Chamber of the Code. This is where he knew he would find the assurance and peace of the King. Midway down the hall he realized that something was amiss. His heart seemed to rise up to his throat. The massive doors of the Chamber were broken in two and lying on the stone floor. It looked as though they had been ripped off their hinges. Gavin's immediate thought was that marauders had taken advantage of the distraction of the hanging and stolen the precious treasure of Chessington.

He quickly grabbed a lamp and ran into the chamber to find the Articles of the Code still in place—untouched. He was relieved and confused at the same time. He studied the parchment with the King's seal to verify that it was indeed the original and not an imitation. Within a few moments, he heard the quickened steps of other knights.

Kifus and another knight entered the chamber with concern on their faces. "What happened here?"

Gavin turned, startled by Kifus's entrance. "I don't know. I've only just arrived myself."

"Thieves?"

He looked at Kifus and saw the same confusion in his countenance that Gavin felt. "Thieves pick locks and steal treasure. They do not tear doors off their hinges and take nothing. This is bizarre."

They walked back to inspect the doors as other knights entered the hall. Kifus knelt down to look closely at the massive hinges that had once held the doors in place. Although the iron hinges were as thick as a man's hand, they were twisted and bent as if made of clay. Gavin knelt as well and ran his hand along the jagged edge of one of the thick doors that was broken in two.

"Who could have the strength to remove these doors in such a fashion?" Gavin asked.

Kifus rubbed his fingers along his forehead. Silence was his only answer. Kifus stood up. "The Articles of the Code are vulnerable to any who enter here. We will post guards for each of the three watches until the doors can be replaced." Kifus posted two knights to stand watch until things settled down and guards could be assigned.

Gavin left the great hall and rode toward home. He was not angry any longer—he was disturbed. ▨

CHAPTER SEVEN

THE PRECIPICE OF PERIL

In the days that followed, Gavin focused on helping Kifus and the other Noble Knights restore some normalcy to Chessington. They had dealt with other fanatics in times past, but none had generated such a strong influence over the people as this stranger. And the Noble Knights had never needed to use such drastic measures to quell the previous fanatics or their disturbances. Like the dissipation of a passing thunderstorm, the knights hoped that the passage of time would calm the people.

Kifus had decided to leave the body of the stranger hanging in the square as a reminder to his followers of their fate should they attempt to continue in their foolhardiness. It seemed to be quite an effective deterrent, for there was nary a trace of the former followers of the stranger.

"Do not look so troubled, Gavin," Kifus said with a smile as they walked toward the great hall early one morning a couple of days after the hanging. "All is as it was, and the streets of Chessington are peaceful once again."

"I find it difficult to believe that it is this easy, Lord Kifus," Gavin said. "Lesser men have had more lasting effects on the people. I don't think we should be too comfortable in our victory."

"Without his charisma and skill," Kifus said, "the peasants this man chose will return to the dirt of peasantry from which they came. Even if they attempt some sort of insurrection, they are no match for the Noble Knights, and we will crush them before it begins." Kifus made a fist to emphasize his point.

Gavin nodded but was not convinced.

As they entered the great hall, many of the knights were already there, and a heightened level of conversation told Gavin that something important had happened.

Gavin walked with Kifus to the head table and watched the men stare at them as though they were hesitant to reveal their information.

"Well, what is it?" Kifus said impatiently.

"The followers have stolen the body," Jayden said.

"And?"

"That is all, Lord Kifus. But it is an insult!" Bremrick said.

Kifus laughed loudly. "Let them have their decaying dead leader. This is no insult. It is a ludicrous attempt to save the minuscule pride of a defunct band of foolish peasants—nothing more." Kifus's laughter seemed to put the knights at ease once again.

But they're gutsy, foolish peasants, Gavin thought.

♛ ♛ ♛

A few weeks passed with little disturbance, and Gavin was still wondering if Kifus was right about the end of the followers.

Shortly thereafter, however, rumors began to circulate within the ranks of the knights that the followers were gathering and meeting in one of the shops near the city's center.

"How do you know this to be true?" Gavin asked of Sir Rolson.

"I have a servant whose son was coerced into joining the followers. My servant is concerned for the boy since he seems increasingly interested in only the teachings of this stranger," Rolson said. "My servant claims that the influence of these heretics is growing, not diminishing, and he wants his son back. I came to you because I knew you would consider the matter seriously. The death of the stranger seems to have lulled many of the knights into complacency, including—"

Gavin held up his hand to stop Rolson from speaking the name. He did not tolerate even the slightest disrespect. He thought for a moment. "I will call for Sir Jayden, and together we will take this to Lord Kifus."

Jayden was eager and more than willing to join Gavin and Rolson to petition Kifus. They met in the great hall and walked to Kifus's residence. He joined them in his greeting room.

Gavin wasted no time. "Lord Kifus, we need to talk to you about—"

"—the secret meetings of the followers?" Kifus interrupted. In an instant Gavin understood that Kifus's apparent lack of interest was nothing more than a ploy to soothe the emotions of the men and the people. There was no hint of complacency in him now.

"I have been watching the followers and their attempt at solidarity since the death of the imposter. It is foolishness, and the time has come for us to end it," Kifus said. "Gavin, tomorrow at dusk assemble twenty knights, and quietly make your way to the large poultry shop just across the south bridge. Do you know of it?"

"I do."

"Warn them and disband them. Use whatever force is necessary, but do so with good judgment."

Gavin nodded.

"For King and Code," Kifus said.

"For King and Code," repeated the three knights.

Upon their return to the great hall, Gavin and Jayden were intercepted by a fellow knight.

"Gentlemen, there is a disturbance at the city square, and I think we should see about it," he said.

Sir Bremrick and a number of other knights joined them as they rode to the city's center. At the edge of the square a crowd was gathering to watch a young man in a sword fight with one of the Noble Knights, Sir Oran. It was an odd scene, for never before had a common citizen of Chessington dared fight one of the chosen knights.

Gavin and the rest of the knights dismounted and approached the altercation, but it did not dissuade the young man from his duel. At first glance it appeared as though the fight would end quickly, for the Noble Knight's attack was relentless. But the young man's sword matched each cut and slice with the skill of an expert.

"I will cut out your insolent tongue, peasant!" the knight said.

"Try as you will, sir, there will be a hundred more to take my place," the young man said defiantly.

The size of the crowd was growing, and Gavin felt a need to get control of the situation.

Jayden whispered into Gavin's ear, "That is Severin, Bremrick's former servant. He is but a peasant."

Gavin glanced toward Bremrick and saw his face redden in anger. He wondered at the skill he'd already seen in the young man.

"What is the meaning of this?" Gavin asked during a pause in the fight.

"This man speaks lies and blasphemies against our King and our Code," Oran said, somewhat winded by the duel.

"My words are upheld by the power of the Prince. The only deception among us is the hypocrisy of the Noble Knights!"

At that, Bremrick cursed and charged upon Severin. He did not fight with finesse, but with sheer brute force. He powered his sword with two hands as he wildly cut at the defense of his former servant. The young man shockingly stood his ground and endured the tremendous blows of his master with the courage of a true nobleman. In Bremrick's recklessness, Gavin saw numerous opportunities for Severin to execute a deadly thrust, but he did not take advantage of them. The fight moved about the edge of the square between trees and shop tables. Bremrick's apparent frustration and inability to defeat this peasant was actually becoming an embarrassment to the knights. Some of the people began to cheer for the young man.

At one point, Gavin stepped forward between Bremrick and the peasant.

"Sir Oran claims that you speak against the King and the Code. Are you a traitor to both?" Gavin asked.

The man drew a deep breath. "I am not!" He turned his back on Bremrick and Gavin and jumped on top of a nearby table. He held his sword up high. "Listen, people of Chessington," he shouted for all to hear. "Many years ago, our King chose a boy to bring about His purpose in this kingdom. Sir Leinad was sold into slavery under the hand of Fairos of Nyland. Our people endured the hardship of his rule until the King called Sir Leinad to deliver them. By the sword of the King, Leinad brought our people out of bondage and into the safety of the Red Canyon. Here many of the people were deceived and despised the King's work and Sir Leinad, for their hearts were weak in the Code. But the King was faithful to His promise and brought them to the beautiful Chessington Valley.

"Once again they were deceived by those who did not abide within the truth of the Code and were carried off into captivity by Lord Kergon and the Kessons. But our great and mighty King did not abandon them, and He brought them out of the land of the Kessons and back to the Chessington Valley to prepare the way of the Chosen One. Today the words of

Sir Leinad that foretold of the King's promise have quickly been forgotten. We have once again fallen under the deception of those who do not understand the true meaning of the Code, for they have both betrayed the King...and murdered His Son!"

Severin pointed his sword toward the Noble Knights, and Gavin felt as though his heart had been pierced by the words of this peasant. The fury of the Noble Knights was unstoppable, and they rushed upon the man with swords drawn. Gavin stood back and felt vindicated as he watched a dozen swords pierce the man at once. But there was no anguish on the young man's face, just a disturbing peaceful countenance.

"The King reigns...and His Son!" he whispered, before falling from the table to the ground dead.

The disorder that followed was more than Gavin or any of the knights could stop. To avoid further incident, they retreated to their mounts and left the square. Gavin feared that the influence of the imposter would soon overwhelm them if they did not act fast.

Such skill and boldness from a peasant! Gavin thought. *And the city is full of peasants. How far will this treachery reach?* He set his course for the home of Lord Kifus.

CHAPTER EIGHT

A KNIGHT'S CRUSADE

 "They may be peasants, but they do not fight as such," Gavin said after telling Kifus about the incident in the square. "They even call themselves Knights of the Prince."

Kifus appeared concerned and angry. "They are not knights. They are followers of a fool! They will no doubt be more wary of us since we have raised our swords against them, but now they also have a martyr to rally them. We must waste no time in crushing them!"

Gavin leaned forward in his chair. The zeal he felt to rid the city of these traitors was powerful. Their opposition to the Noble Knights, the King, and the Code appalled him, and each action he took toward eliminating the Followers confirmed this conviction in his mind.

"Issue an edict against these Followers, and grant me the

authority to search out and eliminate them by whatever means necessary," Gavin said.

Kifus seemed taken with Gavin's aggressive attitude. "So be it! Do not stop until there is no place in all of Chessington for the traitors to hide."

Gavin leaned back in his chair and watched Kifus write a short declaration granting him new powers. Kifus put his seal on the paper and handed it to Gavin.

"Sir Jayden will assist you," Kifus said and dismissed him.

Gavin decided that his raid on the shop near the river would not be a simple warning, for he knew that would be a waste of time. The prison cells of the palace had ample room for the rogue Followers. He selected twenty knights, and Jayden enlisted Bremrick, which did not please Gavin. Bremrick was difficult to control, but considering the recent developments, Gavin decided it was not such a bad choice after all.

At dusk they assembled in the great hall before mounting and riding toward the south bridge. Gavin halted them shy of the bridge, where they secured their steeds before traveling the remaining distance on foot. The sun was now set, and they were able to move through the city streets less noticeably. The smell from burning stoves mixed with the cool air of the approaching night. Gavin heard the ripple of the river's water beneath the bridge.

"There is a large barn behind the shop," Gavin said in a hushed tone. "That is where they gather. Six of you will make your way to the rear of the barn, and the rest of us will enter the front. We will converge together."

Gavin looked into the faces of his men. They were all brave, experienced knights who had committed their lives to defending Chessington. Since their first encounter with the stranger many months ago, they had remained patient and endured humiliation that Noble Knights of the past had never dealt with. Gavin saw the wound of this humiliation in their eyes.

"Tonight we reclaim our honor as Noble Knights," Gavin said. "I want to take them as prisoners, but if they resist, kill them. Our time of mercy is over!"

He led them across the bridge, where six knights separated and maneuvered down an alley to the rear of the barn. Gavin felt the tension in his muscles. He was not used to sneaking up on an enemy. He preferred a straight assault, but that was not an option considering the situation they were facing. He could hear the voices of men and the clashing of swords in training behind the large doors of the barn. It only heightened his apprehension.

Once he had given the six knights time to position themselves, Gavin quietly drew his sword and gripped the handle firmly. The others followed suit and poised themselves for the attack.

Gavin motioned for two knights to open the large doors before them. The doors creaked as they parted, and the sound of clashing swords and accompanying voices hushed to silence. The yellow light from the barn spilled out into the yard and reflected off the gleaming armor of the Noble Knights. Six knights entered through the rear. Gavin quickly counted ten armed Followers standing in the barn and another six standing off to the side with swords still in their scabbards. He had expected many more. A moment of inaction escalated the existing tension.

"You are in violation of Lord Kifus's edict. Drop your swords!" Gavin commanded.

The six men on the side drew their swords, the catalyst that initiated an explosion of sword fighting. Bremrick was the first to attack from the rear, and within a moment the barn and the outer yard were filled with flashing swords, each one bearing the mark of the King.

Gavin brought his sword to bear on what looked like the leader. He did not underestimate the skill of his opponent, and with good reason. Though clearly inexperienced, his opponent's moves were masterful. A slice swished close to Gavin's chest, and he countered with a moulinet that brought his sword through a powerful full-circle attack upon the man. To Gavin's surprise, the man was able to recover from his slice and meet the sword with the flat of his blade. Gavin stepped back and glanced at the other fights. The calm of the city night had been broken by the clash of swords and the grunts of desperate men. He saw one of his knights inflict a deadly thrust on his opponent, and the man fell to the straw floor of the barn. The Noble Knights were overwhelming the Followers, and the man facing Gavin lowered his sword as he too saw the inevitable.

"We yield!" he shouted for all to hear.

Slowly the fighting diminished. Gavin saw Bremrick's opponent lower his weapon, but Bremrick plunged his sword into the man's chest anyway. As the man fell, Gavin saw much more than disdain on Bremrick's face; he saw hatred. Even in battle, Gavin had never seen Bremrick's countenance so contorted with loathing.

Gavin looked directly at Bremrick. "Cease and desist!" he shouted to stop any more needless killing. The Followers lowered their swords, and the knights disarmed them all.

Gavin and his men escorted the Followers and their wounded back to the palace, where they were thrown into cells with common criminals. Jayden assigned extra guards to watch the cells. After meeting with Kifus and relaying the account of the attack, Gavin called for two guards to take the man he had fought into a cell reserved for questioning prisoners.

Gavin entered the cell and looked at the man. His hands were bound behind him, and they had placed him on a wooden stool. There was a large red mark on the man's cheek that hadn't been there earlier.

"What is your name?" Gavin asked.

The man's head was lowered, and his gaze was on the stone floor. "I am William."

"I am sure you have a family…maybe a wife and children? You look to be an intelligent man, William. Denounce your foolishness and your belief in this dead imposter, and I will set you free this very hour," Gavin said. "Lay down your sword, and you can return home to your family. Life will be as it once was."

The man looked up at Gavin. There was a gleam in his eye despite his obvious mistreatment. "The freedom you offer is not freedom at all. Try as you may, you cannot silence the voice of truth. The words of the Prince set men free from the bondage you and the Noble Knights bring."

Gavin was surprised and curious. "How have the Noble Knights brought bondage to the people?"

The man looked into Gavin's eyes as if to discern the sincerity of the question. "True nobility does not come from a man's family name; it is born in his heart. You have created an elite order to keep the Code, yet you isolate the people from it. You train with the sword yet deny the common man the same. The people are kept in poverty so that you may rule over them. This is bondage. You are fearful to lose your power over the people when the real enemy prepares to overtake us. Our only threat to you is the loss of your prestige, and here I sit in fetters to prove it."

"The Noble Knights are the King's guardians of Chessington and His people," Gavin replied. "The people are ignorant of the Code and of the responsibilities of such a duty. Without the Noble Knights they would perish in a day. You were born a peasant, and a peasant you shall die. No teaching of a dead fanatic will ever change that!"

William raised his head. "You are wrong on two counts, sir," he said confidently. "First, truly I was born a peasant, but the Prince has made a knight of me. Second, you do not fight against the teaching of a dead man; you fight against the power of the Prince, who is alive and will return for all of those who choose His path!"

Gavin could not stifle the laugh that echoed throughout the cell. "One thing I *am* wrong about," he said shaking his head. "You are not as intelligent as I took you to be. You are simply another lunatic with delusions of knighthood. Guards! Take this idiot back to his cell!"

The guards lifted him from the stool, and as they walked past Gavin toward the cell door, William looked at Gavin with friendship. "The ways of the Prince are for everyone, even for one such as you."

Gavin grabbed the man's arm. "Why were there only sixteen of you in the barn tonight?"

"We have dispersed, sir. Your murder of Sir Severin was heard of by all...including the Prince."

"Away with him!" Gavin said in disgust. *It is pointless to talk with a crazy man,* he thought.

After that night, Gavin set his mind to eliminating the Followers as quickly and forcefully as possible. He immersed himself in the task, but as the days and weeks passed, he discovered that this challenge was much greater than he had anticipated. He was fighting an elusive enemy who never attacked the Noble Knights in retaliation. With every haven of Followers he routed out, two more would take its place. Eventually the prison cells were full, and the knights had to release some of their captives. Simple management of the prisoners had become an overwhelming task for Kifus and his men. It seemed as though no matter what action Gavin took, the influence and number of the imposter's Followers continued to grow.

Kifus came to rely heavily on Gavin during these dark days. Within a short time, Gavin's skill with the sword and his keen ability to lead the men provided him with the opportunity to rise in position until he was second only to Kifus. Gavin was not arrogant about his position, as other knights often were. In fact, at times he questioned the sincerity of many fellow knights' loyalty to the King and Code. Having been frustrated by the hypocrisy he frequently saw brought a certain measure of disdain for their behavior.

Regardless of how his subordinate knights felt, his heart was set to use all means available to eradicate the kingdom of the blasphemous teachings of this new order of knights begun by the stranger. He did not deny their expertise with the sword, for many a Noble Knight had been defeated by the blade of such traitors, and this was quite a mystery to Gavin. What he did deny was their right to any part of the kingdom under the name of this stranger. He would subdue and kill them all if necessary.

"What action are you taking now, Sir Gavin?" Kifus asked before the assembly of Noble Knights. They had gathered once again in the great hall. Their meetings had become focused entirely on the process of eliminating the Followers. The once important affairs of knighthood had been overshadowed by the eminent threat before them.

Gavin sensed the frustration in Kifus's tone. He stood and addressed the knights. "I have learned that some of the Followers have established training havens outside of Chessington."

"And why is this a threat?" one of the knights asked. "Let

the Outdwellers and the rest of the kingdom deal with their foolish lies. It is no concern of ours."

Gavin shook his head. "It is of great concern to us, for the Followers' focus is still the people of Chessington. If we do not eliminate these new training havens, they will feed those within the city with supplies, people, and weapons," Gavin said. "Lord Kifus, it is paramount that we attack immediately. Grant me men to search out and eliminate these havens. Sir Jayden can continue the work here in the city in my absence."

"Very well, Sir Gavin, you have your men," Kifus said. "A word of warning—remember that your duty is to the citizens of Chessington and no one else. The Outdwellers are not the King's people and therefore no concern of ours. Keep your focus on eliminating this threat to Chessington and to the King's Code. Do not waste your time or resources on anything else. Is that clear?"

"I understand. We will leave in the morning."

As the meeting adjourned, Gavin selected fifteen of the best knights. He visited the garden before retiring to his home. Under the branches of a sprawling shade tree, he sat upon a stone bench and thought about his actions in the past month. He was a different man today. The "messy" work Kifus had assigned to Jayden and Bremrick during the capture of the stranger had now become second nature to Gavin. Somewhere deep in his heart, he regretted having taken up this crusade, for he was becoming what he had once detested.

Is the peace of my heart the price I must pay to restore the order of the Noble Knights and the Code to their rightful place in

Chessington? Gavin suddenly realized that his question might reveal a contradiction he had never considered before. *Why should a peaceful heart be the price of restoring the Code?* He quickly repressed the doubt that was inevitable if he followed such a line of thought. He shook his head as if to clear his mind, then pressed toward home.

CHAPTER NINE

DESPERATE

 The village of Cartelbrook was Gavin's first target. He had received information that the haven there was the first and largest of the outlying sites the Followers were operating from. He knew of two others, but Cartelbrook was the closest. It was also said that the blacksmith there was one of the Followers, and shutting down the supply of swords from his shop was a primary focus for this mission.

The morning light was late to come, for the gray clouds above were thick, which prevented the warmth of the sun from welcoming the day. As Gavin and his knights rode, the dark clouds began to spit droplets of rain. By late morning, he halted his men just prior to a rise in the terrain leading into the village.

Triumph once again seemed agitated and difficult to control. Gavin yanked hard on the reins and the steed settled, but he felt the animal's resistance continually. For years Triumph had been a faithful horse. In battle Gavin had come to rely heavily on the steed, for the horse seemed to know exactly what Gavin required of him in each encounter. In recent months, however, there was no unity or coordination in their actions, and Gavin had begun to consider doing away with Triumph.

"There is no sneaking about today, men," Gavin said, drawing his sword. The sound of fifteen other swords sliding from their scabbards joined his own. "For King and Code!"

"For King and Code!" they echoed.

Gavin and his knights stormed into the village on thundering steeds. The horses' hooves pounded into the wet earthen streets and sprayed a wake of mud in their path. He tried to ignore the terror on the children's faces as the people frantically gathered their young ones to safety. For a moment he felt like they were the marauders he had fought against in years past that had terrorized the citizens of Chessington. He discarded these disturbing thoughts as they descended on the blacksmith's shop and took its owner captive.

Two knights brought him into the street before Gavin.

"Are you a Follower of the imposter of Chessington?" Gavin asked brusquely.

The man was held in the grip of two knights.

"I am a Follower of the Prince," the slender man said. Dark streaks of sweat and rain mixed with soot ran down his cheeks.

"Are you supplying the Followers with swords?" Gavin asked.

The man was silent. One of the knights restraining him hit the man with the back side of his gauntlet, and the man recoiled and winced. Just then, another knight emerged from the shop with a dozen swords bearing the mark of the King. Even though Gavin had expected this, he couldn't control the anger that rose within him. Those swords symbolized the months of turmoil Chessington was now enduring.

"Where are the other Followers?"

The man looked up at Gavin but remained silent.

Gavin's anger deepened. "Destroy the forge and the tools; then burn the shop," he commanded. "Search the other shops and homes. These people are not loyal to Chessington or to the Code. To hide a Follower would be foolish for them. Find them and bring them to me!"

Gavin's analysis proved to be true. The village people were quite willing to reveal the Followers, especially when their families were threatened. Within a short time the knights had gathered another thirty Followers for the prisons of Chessington. There was an occasional fight, but the Noble Knights prevailed in every instance. The captives' hands were bound one to another, and they began their march back to Chessington in the misery of a cold drizzling rain. Gavin was satisfied that the Followers' haven in Cartelbrook had been eradicated.

On the journey home, not far out of Cartelbrook, Gavin led the procession by a farm that was set off the road a fair distance. The house was barely visible through a row of trees that bordered the property.

As they passed, Gavin heard a faint scream and looked toward the farm. An older girl, perhaps a young woman, was running frantically across the field toward the procession of knights and prisoners. She was barefoot and constantly looked behind her as if some horrid beast was about to pounce upon her. Although the rain had now stopped, the ground was wet and muddy. Midway across the field, the girl tripped and fell just as the source of her fear broke through the trees behind her. Two men on horseback pursued the lass at full gallop. The girl screamed hysterically and rose up to continue her flight. Her face, arms, and the front of her dress were covered in mud.

Gavin halted his procession and wondered at the scene unfolding before him. The girl was nearly to Gavin and his men, and the men on horseback were close behind.

"Help me, please—help me!" the girl screamed.

Her eyes were wild with panic. She did not hesitate as she ran straight to him and clutched onto his leg. Triumph spooked slightly, and Gavin tried to settle both his steed and the girl. He looked at the approaching riders, who had slowed their pace since the girl had reached the knights.

As the distance between them closed, Gavin became aware of their daunting size and the manner in which they were arrayed. There was a dark and ominous look about them that he had never seen before. Their horses were large black warhorses that seemed to carry the load of these huge men with ease. The men wore strange armor with broad straps of leather that crossed their breastplates and partly masked an emblem Gavin had never seen. He noticed that the pommel of their swords bore the same mark. Gavin immediately recognized the long handles of the swords still within their scabbards. They were sinister-looking weapons with extra edges that protruded forward from the hilt and base of the blade.

Gavin did not wonder any longer at the fear that obviously gripped the girl.

"Please, sir, don't let them take me!" she pleaded again. Tears streamed down her face.

"Why are they after you?" he asked.

The horsemen were nearly upon them, and the girl spoke quickly. "My father owes them money, but when they came to collect, he could not pay." She began to sob. "They have killed my parents and are taking my brothers and my sister to sell as slaves. Please help us…please!" She clutched Gavin's thigh and tried to hide behind his leg as the massive warriors approached.

The men slowed their steeds to a halt just a few feet from Gavin. He felt small in their presence. They stared at him with disdain and then at the girl beside him.

"What is your business, sirs?" Gavin asked.

The two men did not reply. One of the men moved his horse a few strides off to the right, apparently to get a better look at the knights. Gavin watched the man closely, and he could feel Triumph's hide twitching beneath him. Even Triumph seemed to feel the tension created by these brutes.

Gavin stared into the eyes of the man before him, but his gaze was unnerving. Of all the marauders and powerful men of war he had fought against, he had never seen such daunting warriors as these. He had heard the legends of the existence of such men but considered himself too intelligent ever to believe them.

"It looks like we are in the same business." The warrior spoke in a deep raspy voice.

"These are not slaves; they are criminals," Gavin replied.

"So I've heard," the man said and smiled wickedly at the other warrior. "Chains will suit them well," he said wryly. "Give us the girl, and you can be on your way."

"Please…please…no…" The girl whispered to Gavin.

"Where are you from and what is your business with the girl?" Gavin asked.

The other man had rejoined his partner. Both men stared fiercely at Gavin.

"That is not your concern," the leader said. "It would be well for you to do as I say, or your ride to Chessington will end here!"

The other warrior's hand came to rest on his sword. Gavin was amazed at their arrogance, for he commanded a force of fifteen brave knights and there were only two of them. However, he could not deny a sense of insignificance both in stature and in force. He wondered if perhaps more warriors were waiting in the trees. As the tension mounted, he remembered Kifus's words of warning and his responsibility. Additionally, he was in no position to battle any sizable force with his prisoners under guard. If he chose to fight, he could very well lose not only some of his prisoners, but also the lives of some of his men.

"I am bound by the Code to protect the citizens of Chessington." He looked down at the pleading eyes of the girl momentarily, and he felt even smaller. "The affairs of Outdwellers are not the affairs of the Noble Knights," he said and turned his eyes away from the girl.

One of the warriors dismounted and walked toward the

girl. She screamed and clutched Gavin's leg, pleading all the while. Triumph turned his head toward the girl as if to shelter her. Something was wrong and Gavin felt sick. Fear, duty, humiliation, and responsibility pulled his heart in all different directions as the dark warrior grabbed one of the girl's arms and ripped her away from Gavin's leg.

"No!" she screamed, reaching for something—someone—to grab on to.

The warrior dragged her to his horse and threw her onto the front of his saddle facedown. He mounted behind her and turned back toward the farm. The other warrior lingered a moment, again seeming to evaluate Gavin. He smiled in a way that gave Gavin chills, then turned to follow his companion back to the farm.

Gavin resumed their march to Chessington.

"Who were they?" one of the knights riding next to Gavin asked.

Gavin only shook his head. He did not speak the rest of the journey home, for he could not overcome the sickening feeling that emanated from the pit of his stomach and filled his whole body and spirit with sorrow. All that had once made him a proud and gallant knight seemed to be vanishing. He blamed the Followers for destroying his life, for all the evil that had befallen him.

The dark clouds above released another load of rain upon them as they rode, and Gavin ached for peace in his heart…a peace that now seemed so elusive.

That evening, Leisel came to Gavin and soothed his tormented heart with soft words of assurance and a gentle touch upon his arm. But every time he closed his eyes, the desperate, dirty face of a peasant girl was pleading with him to save her. He looked for the temporary peace that sleep usually held, but even his dreams refused to give him solace.

CHAPTER TEN

DARK STEEL

Gavin continued to pursue the Followers like a prowling lion, and his methods became more harsh with each passing week. In his quiet moments, however, the seed of doubt grew. The more it grew and plagued his mind, so grew the fierceness of his persecution of the Followers. The sheer momentum of his actions would not allow a different course now, and his crusade to exterminate every Follower turned into an obsession. They feared Gavin more than any other knight, even Bremrick. It was a passion that overwhelmed him, yet with each step the gnawing teeth of doubt tore at his heart. His sleep became filled with restless fits of fragmented visions...visions of a man hanging on a tree and of a peasant being pierced by the swords of enraged men.

Gavin's visits to the Chamber of the Code no longer brought him peace as they once had. But he could not—would not—turn aside from what he knew to be right, for he was Sir

Gavin, defender of the Code, servant of the King, and judge of the traitorous Followers. He believed that his peace lay at the end of his successful crusade to eliminate the memory of the imposter and his Followers from Chessington.

On this day, Gavin was leading an entourage of Noble Knights out of Chessington to the east toward Denrith, another haven for the Followers. The journey would take most of the day, and he hoped to arrive before nightfall. At midday, Gavin halted his men in the shade of some towering trees that seemed to stand guard over a small forest ahead. It was a welcome reprieve from the humid heat of the day.

"Sir Hanan, dismount the men. I will survey the road ahead," Gavin commanded.

"Yes sir."

Gavin galloped ahead into the beauty of an intriguing forest. After a few moments, he slowed his steed to a trot and finally to a walk. The air was much cooler here, and Gavin felt the burden of his task lift slightly as he enjoyed the splendor of vibrant forest flowers, the smell of evergreens, and the lilting sound of a brook not far off. The main road pressed on through the forest directly ahead, but a less traveled path diverted to the left, and Gavin assumed it ended at the brook he heard. It was a peaceful invitation away from the drudgery of a long journey. Triumph instinctively followed the path toward the water, and Gavin allowed the diversion.

Within a short time, he arrived in a clearing at the brook and dismounted to allow his horse time to quench his thirst. Gavin did the same, for the water was cool and refreshing.

A moment later, Triumph became startled and Gavin instantly felt the tension in the horse. He grabbed the reins to keep the animal from bolting.

"Easy, Triumph," he said to calm the animal, but the horse's fear only intensified. Gavin looked about and saw nothing unusual, but he thought it best to mount and vacate the area for Triumph's sake. As he did so, his steed turned to face the north, and Gavin could not seat his foot in the stirrup.

"What's wrong with you, Triumph?" He was becoming agitated once again with the horse. "Keep this up and you'll be pulling a plowshare. Now settle down!"

He pulled hard on the reins and grabbed the saddle. As he placed a foot in the stirrup, the steed reared up. Gavin was thrown clear of the frightened animal and landed a few paces to the side. Triumph bolted back up the path, leaving Gavin bruised and angry.

I am through with that horse! Gavin thought. He would find a new mount by week's end.

Gavin stood and was thankful for no broken bones, for it was a violent throw. In an instant, however, he realized the source of fear that his steed had perceived. Five fierce-looking warriors broke through the forest wall into the clearing, riding massive warhorses. He had seen their like only once before in his life, on the road from Cartelbrook.

Gavin was in awe once again at their size and form. He became overwhelmed with dread. The massive black steeds were not too large for their riders. They approached Gavin with an air of authority, power, and arrogance. One of the men walked his horse straight to Gavin and stopped just short of overrunning him. Gavin did not dare back away lest he show his mounting fear. The hot breath of the knight's beast permeated the surrounding air, and Gavin was forced backward one step as the animal shook his head up and down near Gavin's face. The other riders slowly moved to flank their leader.

Gavin knew that these men were not mere thieves or marauders. There was something distinctly unnatural and evil about them.

"What have we stumbled upon here?" the man asked with a wry grin. His voice was raspy and deep. There was not a hint of relief in this picture of evil that stood before Gavin.

"Perhaps a frightened forest squirrel, eh, Sir Devinoux?" replied one of the men with a guttural laugh.

Gavin wanted desperately to draw his sword for some security, but he was sure the action would bring death, so he stayed his hand. He needed to discover their intention before he succumbed to his instinct to fight these brutes.

"No, Sir Vicis, this is not a forest squirrel." The leader's face showed a moment of enlightenment. "This one I know. He does the bidding of our commander. This is Sir Gavin of Chessington—our ally!"

The roar of laughter from the circle of brutes echoed through the forest and brought its inhabitants to silence. Gavin was disgusted and insulted.

"Who is your commander?" Gavin asked.

The five men slowly dismounted. Gavin was a full head shorter than any of the warriors.

"Don't you know?" the leader replied. "Your work is highly praised by him, Gavin." He spoke Gavin's name with such disdain that Gavin shuddered.

Gavin's hand moved toward his sword.

"Lord Lucius is pleased with your work, Noble Knight!"

Gavin could refrain no longer, even if it meant his death. The insult to his honor was more than he could bear. He quickly unsheathed his sword and held it before the brute. None of the men responded or even seemed the slightest bit alarmed.

"Withdraw your insults and stand aside!" Gavin commanded.

The leader glared at Gavin for a moment with eyes of dark steel. "You are an ignorant fool, Arrethtraen knave! Draw your sword on Devinoux, and you will die!"

The blurred motion of the warrior's sword stunned Gavin. His sword was nearly blown from his hand on the first clash, and it was all Gavin could do to maintain his grip. There was no offensive counter, just defense and retreat. The warrior's attacks were powerful and relentless. One dominant blow slammed into Gavin's sword and moved its protection clean away from his chest. The warrior seized the opportunity to recoil and thrust his blade clear through Gavin's right shoulder until the shorter edges of the sword began to penetrate his chest as well. Gavin screamed in agony and instantly lost the grip on his sword. His body convulsed from the steely invasion and his legs began to buckle, but the warrior held his sword up—still lodged in Gavin's shoulder—to prevent Gavin from falling.

Devinoux grabbed Gavin and pulled him farther onto the blade and close to his face. "Lord Lucius will be disappointed to lose such an effective puppet, but he will find another. The kingdom is full of fools such as you!"

Gavin barely noticed the stench of the warrior's breath, for he was edging close to unconsciousness in this excruciatingly painful position.

The warrior abruptly withdrew his sword, and Gavin collapsed to the forest floor beside his useless weapon. The five warriors encircled Gavin with drawn swords to kill their victim in a semiritualistic sacrifice. Their faces held the sadistic and dark smiles of evil souls.

Gavin was afraid, confused, and powerless. The purpose of his life and the quest of his journey seemed all wrong here at his final moments. *My King…I have given my life for Your honor. Why am I so empty in the end?*

The evil warriors held their swords high above Gavin, and he readied himself for his final breath.

The neigh of a horse echoed through the forest trees. Although Gavin could not see the steed or his rider, he could see the stark fear that lit upon the faces of his executioners. *Has an army come to save me?* He was sure that only an army could frighten these brutes.

The dark warriors abandoned their execution of Gavin and took defensive positions to face the apparent threat. One man rode into the clearing atop a gallant white steed. The horse reared, and the streaks of sunlight that penetrated through the forest trees gleamed off the shining silver armor of this nobleman.

"Not Him!" Gavin heard one of the warriors say.

"He is alone," the leader replied sharply, but this did not seem to assuage the warriors' obvious fear.

The rider dismounted and walked toward the gruesome line of dark warriors. The guard on His helmet was raised, and Gavin wondered if perhaps this was their leader, for He had not drawn His sword and did not appear fearful at all. He soon realized this was a false assumption, however, when the warriors raised their swords and began to spread apart to form a semicircle about the man.

"Leave at once!" the powerful voice commanded.

The leader of the dark warriors sneered. "You are severely outnumbered, fool. If I were to kill You, my power would become great."

There was a moment of silence as the five brutes finalized their positions around the gallant knight. They all attacked Him at once. In the blink of an eye, the man drew His sword, defended a cut from the nearest threat, and thrust His sword through the chest of one of the warriors. In a blur of motion, His sword flew to meet the onslaught of powerful blades.

Gavin was in awe. After the first warrior fell, he could see that the others were hesitant to fully commit to the fight, as though they knew that the next closest would fall as quickly as the first. After another quick parry and thrust, Gavin heard a scream as the man's majestic sword penetrated another warrior's upper arm, causing him to drop his grisly weapon and back away from the fight.

The fight paused, and the leader looked at his wounded comrades. The other two warriors took a step back.

"Fight Him, you cowards!" he yelled.

They lowered their swords. "You fight Him," one of them replied.

The leader cursed and stepped back. "Get them on their horses!" he said and pointed to the two wounded warriors lying on the ground.

"We are not finished with You!" the leader said.

The man raised His chin slightly. "Of that you can be sure!"

After a few moments, the dark warriors disappeared into the forest, and the clearing became peaceful once again. Gavin's pain seemed to increase as the tension of the situation abated.

The man came to Gavin and stood over him. "Gavin, why do you fight against Me?"

"Who are You that I have offended, my Lord?" Gavin looked on the noble form of his deliverer and felt ashamed and insignificant, for this man was clearly of royal blood that transcended any man born in Arrethtrae.

"I am He whom you persecute daily. I am He whom you wounded and killed," the knight said as He removed His helmet. "I am the Prince, the Son of the King of Arrethtrae!"

Gavin stared at the man in shock. *How can this be?* he wondered. Had he too already passed the doors of death? The pain in his body reminded him that he was indeed alive, and yet he knew within his heart that this man before him truly was the Prince they had killed. The last time Gavin had seen Him, His face was beaten and bruised, but now there was only a countenance that radiated true nobility and royalty. The pain in Gavin's arm was momentarily forgotten as he searched for words and found none.

The Prince knelt beside him, and Gavin tried to retreat into the dirt beneath him. He trembled, not for fear of what the Prince would do, but for the recognition of his own misdirected life.

"Look into My eyes, Gavin," the Prince said. "I have been calling you. The peace you seek you will find if you follow Me."

Gavin looked into the Prince's eyes for the first time and fully understood what Demus had said about Him. He felt as though his soul had been split open for the entire kingdom to see. He was ashamed, humbled, and excited all at once.

"My Prince!" Gavin whispered.

The Prince placed a hand on Gavin's shoulder. "Go to the house of Sir Chadwick. He will tend to your wound."

"What am I to do?"

"Be still, Gavin…be still."

Gavin could hear the distant sound of horses approaching. The Prince mounted His majestic white steed and gazed once more at Gavin before riding into the forest and disappearing.

"Sir Gavin!" Hanan shouted as he halted his men short of where Gavin lay.

The pain intensified once again, and Gavin winced as he

tried to rise to a sitting position. The grass and leaves beneath him were stained bright crimson from his blood.

"Who did this to you?" Hanan scanned the surrounding trees. He quickly assigned four men to search the area.

"I don't know."

Hanan removed Gavin's tunic and quickly began to bandage his wound. The bleeding was profuse, and Hanan looked worried.

"Take me to the house of Chadwick in Denrith," Gavin struggled to say.

"But sir, that is the place of the Followers we seek to destroy. We must get you back to Chessington."

Gavin grabbed Hanan's tunic. "No! Denrith is closer. Take me to Chadwick. That is an order!"

Hanan hesitated. "Can you ride? We found Triumph."

"Yes," Gavin replied weakly, but the loss of blood was great and unconsciousness was near.

After an attempt to mount him on his horse, Gavin was instead placed on a cot behind Triumph. Gavin fought to stay awake to ensure that their journey continued toward Denrith and not Chessington. He had never been more miserable in his life as he endured the excruciating pain in his shoulder— and in his soul. Anguished hallucinations haunted him.

What have I done? he asked himself. *What have I done?*

CHAPTER ELEVEN

BETWEEN TWO WORLDS

When Gavin awoke, three men across the room were talking in hushed tones. He remained still.

"His presence here threatens us all, Chadwick," said one of the men. He was a strong, stocky fellow with a full beard.

"I had no choice. The other Noble Knights did not want to leave him here, but he insisted. I fear I would be in chains and on my way to a prison cell were it not for his insistence that I treat him."

"Will he recover?" asked the youngest of the three men. There was genuine concern in his voice. Although he wore the clothes of a peasant, the other two men did not treat him as such.

"I'm not sure. The wound is severe, and he has lost a lot of blood. Whatever the outcome, we have been discovered and you can be sure that the Noble Knights will return," Chadwick replied.

The stocky man turned and paced to the door and back while rubbing his forehead. "I don't like this—not at all!" he said as he looked at his two friends.

"I don't think we're in immediate danger, Sir Bensen," the young man said. "For now we must do everything we can to keep him alive."

Chadwick took a deep breath and then paused.

"What is it, Chadwick?" the younger man asked.

"He claims to have…"

"To have what?" Bensen said, nervous and impatient.

"To have seen the Prince."

The moment of silence was indicative of the astonishment they all felt.

Bensen shook his head. "No…no…this is a ruse to capture us all! Weston, you are wrong. We are all in very grave danger!"

"What if he is telling the truth?" the younger man named Weston asked.

Bensen looked at Weston fiercely. He pointed in Gavin's direction. "This is Sir Gavin, the Tyrant of Chessington, we are talking of. I would not be surprised if he fell on his own sword just to gain our confidence so he could destroy us all!"

The Tyrant of Chessington? Gavin cringed and closed his eyes tightly.

Chadwick rubbed his beard. "What are we to do with him then?"

"We cannot kill him, for it is not the way of the Prince, but nothing prevents us from leaving him here. His men will return, and by then we will be long gone," Bensen said.

Weston shook his head. "Gentlemen, this man could be a true Follower of the Prince, and we must believe him."

"And risk condemning ourselves and our families to the prisons and torture chambers of the Tyrant?" Bensen asked incredulously.

"I will take him to Cresthaven," Weston said.

Chadwick and Bensen stared at Weston in silence. Chadwick placed a hand on Weston's shoulder. "Sir Weston, you have proven yourself both wise and brave as a Knight of the Prince, but I cannot help but consider this a foolish decision. If you are wrong, you will be sacrificing your wife and children to the prisons, and you will very likely be killed."

"If I trust this man and ill fortune befalls me and my family, then I am guilty of too much trust and can stand before the Prince in honor. But if I do not trust him and his heart is true, then I will have turned my back on a brother and on the Prince. My honor will have forsaken me. I choose the former, for I believe in the Prince and in His power to transform the hearts of men…even the heart of the Tyrant of Chessington."

After a brief moment of contemplation, Bensen spoke. "So be it. We must get Chadwick and his family away from here immediately."

"Agreed," Weston replied. "Whether this man speaks the truth or not, his men will eventually be back for him."

Bensen turned to Chadwick. "Prepare your family. I will return shortly with help."

"The King reigns," Chadwick said.

"And His Son," replied Weston and Bensen in unison.

Gavin tried to move his arm and moaned in pain.

Weston came to him. "How are you feeling, Sir Gavin?"

Gavin looked at Weston and marveled. Though he was dressed as a peasant, there was nobility in his stature. Gavin wore the splendid clothes and armor of the Noble Knights and yet felt small next to Weston. He knew he could trust him, for his dark blue eyes were full of compassion. Weston's hair was dark brown and slightly wavy. His chin was square and accurately characterized the confidence of the man. He knelt down to inspect Gavin's shoulder.

"I am…wounded," he said, speaking more of his heart than of his shoulder.

Weston paused and looked into Gavin's eyes, then nodded. "Had the sword been a bit lower, you would probably be dead. We can be thankful for that."

Gavin grasped Weston's arm, and he winced from the pain the movement caused. "I am thankful for the trust of one man."

"And that you have. We must prepare you for a journey out of Denrith. It could be a very difficult one for you considering your condition."

"I understand," Gavin said. "The large fellow's concern is not unwarranted. I don't think my men will return to Chessington without me. It would be a disgrace, for in their eyes I am now either a hostage or a traitor. Either way, Lord Kifus will insist that they recover me."

Bensen returned with six other men, and they wasted no time in their preparations to abandon Chadwick's home. Within a short time, the residence was empty, and Chadwick and his family had disappeared into the community of Denrith as common citizens.

During this time, Weston tended Gavin's wound and prepared him for the journey ahead. This proved quite difficult, for his dressings needed to be changed and the pain that accompanied any movement was nearly unbearable. It radiated from his shoulder throughout his entire body, and his right arm felt as though it were on fire.

Bensen stayed behind to help Weston, but he was clearly apprehensive. Out behind Chadwick's home a two-wheeled cart was configured to carry Gavin on a makeshift bed. Triumph did not resist the rigging and patiently waited for Weston and Bensen to set Gavin on the cart behind him.

Both Weston and Bensen became concerned when a man on horseback galloped down the alley and did not slow his horse until he was nearly upon them. It was one of the men who had earlier helped evacuate Chadwick and his family.

"The Noble Knights are returning!"

"I knew it!" Bensen said.

"We can't outrun them, and he would not survive the flight," Weston said.

The rider looked back from where he had come. "They are

on the outskirts of the city and riding quickly. We have only a few moments!"

"Get him to Eagle Pass, and I will gather the men and meet you there. The passage is narrow enough to fend them off," Bensen said. "If we can hold them, you should be safe. They would have to ride for miles to find another way through."

Weston grabbed Bensen's forearm. "I thought you didn't believe him."

Bensen squinted his eyes, and the look of battle was in him. "I don't—but I believe you, and I am praying that you are right. Now go!"

Weston mounted his horse and grabbed Triumph's reins. Gavin saw Bensen look down at him. There was a measure of consternation on his face, and the pain in Gavin's heart deepened. Here was a man who was putting his life and the lives of others on the line for him when just a day ago Gavin would have gladly had him beaten and thrown in prison. Nothing he could say or do would justify his past or convince this man of his gratefulness.

Weston quickly rode up the alley, leading Triumph by the reins, with Gavin in tow on the cart. Gavin could hear Bensen giving the messenger orders as they departed.

Every jostle of the cart brought agonizing pain to Gavin. At times it felt as though the sword was still embedded in his shoulder. Gavin raised his head to look behind them, but thus far no one followed them. They cleared the limits of the city and entered the woods that bordered to the north. The road became rough, and Gavin thought he might lose consciousness simply from the pain. He sensed an increase in the elevation of the terrain. From what he could see, the surrounding landscape was becoming a rugged mixture of trees and large rock outcroppings. After a few moments he heard the sound of many galloping horses.

The road straightened in a small clearing at the edge of the woods just prior to the entrance to the pass. Hanan and the rest of the Noble Knights soon appeared behind them in full pursuit with swords drawn. Weston saw them too and increased Triumph's speed. Gavin wondered if he would survive the pounding of the cart. The Noble Knights gained on them quickly, and it looked as though their flight would be cut short. He heard Weston slap Triumph's hindquarter and yell as he drew his sword. Weston quickly circled his steed and faced the Noble Knights single-handedly. Triumph raced onward without a guide. Gavin knew that Weston would never survive such a gallant encounter, but just before they met, a dozen mounted men burst from the woods on one side of the clearing to join Weston in the fight. The two forces collided and the sound of crashing steel upon steel filled the air.

Weston engaged Hanan. In that brief encounter, Gavin saw the skill of an expert swordsman in his new friend.

"Get him through the gorge" Bensen yelled to Weston, "and we will hold them off here."

Weston pulled back, turned his horse around, and galloped to catch Gavin and Triumph.

The rugged trail narrowed, and the rocky pass towered high on each side. Gavin could see Bensen and his men defending the entrance to the pass as the Noble Knights fought aggressively to break through. A gentle curve in the road caused the rocky walls of the pass to obscure Gavin's sight as the sound of neighing horses and clashing swords slowly diminished behind them.

There was no turning back now. In that moment, he knew that he had severed all ties to his former life. Gavin was no longer a Noble Knight, and the life before him seemed as uncertain as the rugged terrain that surrounded him.

CHAPTER TWELVE

NO MORE
A KNIGHT

After a great distance of harsh travel, Gavin finally felt the horses slowing. He opened his eyes to see Weston looking back to confirm that there was no pursuit by the Noble Knights. He hoped that Weston's friends were able to not only deter their pursuers, but escape themselves. Gavin was pale and barely coherent. His bandage was soaked with blood. As Weston attended to his wound, the warm and friendly arms of unconsciousness enveloped Gavin.

Gavin awoke just enough to sense his misery. His world seemed to bend and shift as he tried to focus his mind, but he could not stop the apparent delusions. He sensed wetness in his mouth and tried to swallow, but it required great effort. He could just make out two dark figures standing over him.

"This is the man?" he heard a hollow voice say.

"Yes," replied the other form. "Fever has set in...there is nothing else I can do. I fear he shall die."

"If it were not the Prince Himself who told me, I would not believe it."

Gavin felt unconsciousness beginning to swallow him again.

"Told you what?"

"He gave this to me. You are to apply it to his wound. It should save his life. He told me that this man is chosen. For the sake of the Prince he will suffer many things and…"

The figures slowly disappeared into the blackness along with the words that Gavin could no longer hear.

The voices seemed so small and distant, like footsteps echoing down a long hallway. He was sure they were real, but Gavin couldn't quite understand the words. The fog was lifting, but only very slowly.

"Why do you suppose Papa brought him here?" one small voice said.

"I don't know. I heard him talking to Mother about the Noble Knights."

Gavin opened his eyes and the voices stopped. He wondered where he was. It took him a moment to remember why his shoulder was so painful.

He turned his head to look about the unfamiliar room. Every motion took monumental effort. The room was quite large for a bedroom. The tall ceiling was comprised of intricate inlaid tiles and ornate moldings. There were white columns at the doorway and at the large window on the opposite side of the room. The curtains and tapestries looked older and not quite fitting for a room that appeared to have been designed for regal and expensive adornments. His eyes came to rest on two children standing a few feet from his bed.

"See, I told you he wasn't dead," said the little girl to a younger boy, who was standing partly behind her.

Gavin took a deep breath, and it felt as though it was the first his lungs had ever taken. "Hi there," he managed to whisper.

The little girl smiled. Her nose and cheeks were dotted with freckles, and her dark brown eyes matched the long brown hair that hung to her waist.

"You sure have been sleeping a long time, sir," she said.

Gavin tried to move, but even his good limbs protested with stiffness. He managed to rise up on his left elbow.

"How long have I been sleeping, little miss?" he asked.

"It's been six days since Papa first brought you here. Keaton thought you were dead because you were lying so still," the little girl said.

"I see." Gavin figured the little boy had almost been right. "What's your name, little miss?"

"I'm Adelaide, but everyone calls me Addy. This is Keaton."

The little boy lowered his eyes and tried to hide farther behind his big sister. Unlike his sister, his face was free of freckles, and he had blond hair that looked as fine as silk.

"Papa says you saw the Prince. Is that true?" Addy asked with big eyes.

"Yes it is, although I'm not sure why He saved my life."

Addy's smile vanished, and she looked perplexed. "You don't know much about the Prince, do you?"

"No, Addy, I don't. In fact, I don't know much about anything anymore. That which I thought was right is wrong. And that which I thought was wrong is true. I believed the Prince to be an imposter, when in truth, I was the imposter all along."

Addy looked as though she was thinking hard about his words.

"What do you know about the Prince?" he asked.

"I know that He doesn't kill people; He saves them. And I know that He did so many wonderful things that all the parchment in the kingdom could not contain them."

"That's a lot of wonderful things," Gavin said with a smile.

"Yes it is, and I know something else"—Addy smiled back—"He likes children… Do you?"

Gavin dropped his head, and his gaze went to the floor as he remembered all the terrorized little faces of the children whose fathers and mothers he had taken and put in prison. He did not think his heart could ache any more than it already did, but the honest and innocent comments of this little girl found a corner of his heart to prick.

"I've never had a chance to try," he said sadly and managed a weak smile.

"What a sad place you must come from…a place with no children to like."

Gavin's remorse overwhelmed him, and he found it difficult to swallow or talk. He felt his eyes beginning to tear up.

Keaton pulled on Addy's sleeve and leaned over to whisper in her ear. Gavin took another deep breath and gathered his composure.

"Keaton wants to know what it feels like to be stabbed with a sword."

"Well, Keaton, I hope you will never find out, for it is very painful," he said, grateful for a different topic.

Weston entered the room. "I see our friend has awoken."

He walked to the children and gave them a hug.

"Have you been bothering Sir Gavin?" he asked Addy.

"No, Papa. I was just telling him about the Prince."

"I see. Why don't you run along and tell your mother that Sir Gavin is awake?"

"All right," Addy replied, and the two children ran out the door.

Weston walked over to Gavin's bed. "How are you feeling?"

Gavin noticed that Weston was no longer in the peasant clothes he had worn in Denrith. He had on the garb of a knight. Gavin suddenly became aware of his intense hunger.

"Like I've just returned from the dead," Gavin said.

"We were concerned you would not make it. You lost a great deal of blood, and the ride on the cart was too much for you. It will take some time to regain your strength."

Gavin looked at Weston and was humbled. Here was a man who had risked his life and was now risking the lives of his family to save an enemy. *Is this the way of the Prince?* This went beyond any code he understood.

"Thank you, Sir Weston," he said.

Weston smiled. A lovely woman entered the room and came to stand beside him.

"Marie, this is Sir Gavin of Chessington. Sir Gavin, this is Marie, my wife," Weston said.

"I am pleased to meet you, my lady. Please forgive me if I do not rise. I fear my legs would fail me."

"I am pleased to meet you, sir," Marie said. "Welcome to our home."

"There are no words to express my gratitude. You have saved my life with your kindness, and I am greatly indebted to you."

Marie smiled, "Our home is your home. You must be famished. I will bring some food for you."

Gavin tried not to ravenously devour the food, but he could not remember being this hungry in his life. His shoulder felt better, although it was still nearly impossible to move his arm. He was thankful that the intense burning sensation was gone.

A few days passed, and Gavin's wound continued to heal, but the strength of his arm did not return. The best he could do was form a weak fist with his hand and raise it to his waist. One day, he tried to grasp the hilt of his sword and lift it, but the sheer weight caused him to lose his grip, and the sword fell to the ground. He knelt to the floor to pick it up and hesitated. He ran his fingers along the fine blade and became downhearted. Although his physical wound was healing, the wound in his heart seemed only to worsen.

"With this sword I wrought devastation when I believed I

was bringing justice—for the King, no less!" he whispered. Gavin closed his eyes and shook his head. Nothing made sense anymore. His perfect world had come to an end, and all that was left was an empty shell of a man. *Was it pride that lured me into playing the part of a zealous fool?* he wondered. He clung to the vision of the Prince, for it was the only lanyard that kept him from complete despondency.

Weston entered the room. "Are you all right, Gavin?" He knelt beside him.

"I, uh, dropped my sword. I don't think I would be much good in a fight right now."

Weston helped him to his feet. "Are you up for a walk?"

"I think that would be good." Some fresh air would help him feel better.

Weston's home was much more than a country cottage; it was a beautiful large manor nestled in the rolling hills of the countryside near the Wickmere River. Evidence of former grandeur was everywhere. It would require many servants and groundskeepers to maintain such an estate properly, but Gavin noticed that the only current occupants were Weston, Marie, and their two children. As a result, the less important aspects of the estate had fallen into disrepair both inside and out. Gavin later learned that much of Weston's wealth was being used to support the Followers in Chessington and in the surrounding regions.

The sky was beautiful and bright blue, and the smell of honeysuckle and wildflowers filled the air. Becoming absorbed in the lush country diminished the anguish of Gavin's past...at least for a time. After a long walk about the estate, they arrived at the stables. They entered Triumph's stall, and Weston began to groom the horse.

"What a magnificent animal you have here," Weston said.

"I used to think so, but he has become more and more difficult to control. He has resisted me for some time now. He, along with the rest of the kingdom, seems to be against me."

"Perhaps your horse is wiser than you." Weston looked up and smiled.

Gavin accepted the teasing, but then considered the bizarre possibility that Triumph had actually understood his folly while he was fighting against the Prince and His Followers.

"He is not an Arrethtraen horse, that's for sure," Weston said as he combed the steed's mane.

"Not Arrethtraen? I've never heard of a horse that wasn't. Why do you say that?" Gavin asked.

"The extra folds inside his ears—have you ever noticed them?"

"Yes, but I assumed them to be a defect of some sort," Gavin said.

"They are no defect." Triumph allowed them to inspect his ears. "Ever ridden him at night or in thick fog?"

Gavin thought for a moment and realized that on such occasions the other knights had struggled to keep up with him, and he and Triumph had usually led the way, even when Kifus was commanding.

"A horse like Triumph has the ability to navigate the terrain even when it is impossible to see. He is a special horse. How did you come by him?"

"It is an odd story," Gavin said as he reached to stroke Triumph, but the horse raised his head up and away from his hand as if to refuse his touch. Gavin shook his head.

"I was raised by my mother in a home on the outskirts of Chessington. My father was a Noble Knight but was killed in battle when I was just an infant. My mother did the best she could, and when I was old enough she arranged for me to be a squire under Kifus, who had trained under my father for some time. One evening, when I was still a boy, a large fellow came to our home asking for food. It was raining heavily, and he was soaked to the bone. He looked weary, so my mother showed pity and invited him to eat supper with us, even though I could tell she was very nervous about letting him into our home. He did not carry a sword or any weapon that I could see, but when he took off his drenched cloak and stood straight I was amazed at his size. He said he was just passing through the city on his way to a distant land. He was a quiet fellow, so my mother did most of the talking through the meal. He seemed genuinely interested in all she said."

Gavin paused as he thought of his mother.

"She talked more about my father that night than I had ever heard before or since. After the meal, my mother offered the man a place to sleep in the stable, and he accepted. We quartered his horse and a colt he had with him. In the morning, we fed him breakfast, and he prepared to leave. Before he did, though, he put the colt's reins in my mother's hand and said, 'The compassion of One heals many sorrows.' My mother tried to refuse his gift, but he would not allow it. The man mounted his horse and then looked at me. 'Take good care of Triumph, and he will take good care of you,' he said. I never understood why the man felt as though he needed to give us a colt in exchange for a meal and a straw bed, but I was grateful. Triumph trained well, and he brought great success to me as the mighty horse of a Noble Knight. He saved my life on more than one occasion."

Gavin paused. He tried to make a fist with his right hand and then looked to the ground.

"Now I am no longer a Noble Knight, and neither am I a Knight of the Prince. My cause has left me, and my heart is empty but for the grief that swells with each passing hour for my offenses against the King, the Prince, and His people. My sword is not what I thought it to be, and the strength of my arm has abandoned me. Even Triumph seems to understand that I am nothing but a pauper now."

Weston looked on Gavin with compassion and smiled, but Gavin's sadness deepened even further.

"Do you delight in my demise, Weston?" Gavin asked. "Although…I cannot condemn you, for I deserve much more than a vengeful smile from a former foe."

Weston shook his head. "No, Gavin. I do not delight in your demise. I delight in your heart, for everyone who is to follow the Prince must first understand his own unworthiness. He must first understand that he is indeed a pauper."

Weston placed a firm hand on Gavin's good shoulder.

"You are in the place of beginnings, my friend. Few find it, but now you are not far from beginning your new life in service to the King, the Prince, and the Code."

Gavin was confused, for Weston seemed to talk in riddles. He was not comforted, and the memories of his past continued to haunt him.

Over the next few days, a friendship grew between the men, and Gavin found opportunity to further enjoy the company of Adelaide and Keaton. Their joyful presence often left him smiling. The children entreated him to join in a number of their games. With each passing day he became fonder of the children. Weston talked frequently of the Prince, and the veil of deception was slowly lifting from Gavin's mind, although he was becoming impatient with his healing. The zeal within his soul was awakening again, and he could not find peace on the bed of recovery.

Late one bright afternoon, Gavin and Weston were walking beside a row of mature elm trees that framed the front courtyard of Cresthaven. A rider on horseback approached the men. Gavin had never seen him before, but Weston did not seem alarmed.

"Sir Nias! It is good to see you again," Weston said as the man halted his horse and dismounted.

Gavin recognized the mark of the Prince on his tunic.

"And you, Sir Weston. I see your patient is in better condition than when I last saw him," Nias replied.

"Sir Gavin, this is Sir Nias of Denrith."

Gavin bowed. "I am pleased to meet you, sir."

"Were it not for Nias, you probably would have died, Gavin," Weston said.

Gavin was confused, for he was sure he had never seen this man before.

"Nias arrived at Cresthaven just when we thought we were losing you to the fever. He brought a salve to apply to your wound that broke the fever," Weston explained.

Gavin turned to Nias. "Then I am indeed indebted to you and all the more pleased to have met you, sir, that I may some-day repay your good service to me."

"I am not the one to thank, sir, for I had little to do with your recovery. I was simply a messenger."

"Can you join us for supper?" Weston asked Nias.

"Thank you, but I must decline your kind offer. I have come to deliver a message, and then I must be on my way." Nias turned to Gavin and looked at him as though he was unsure if he should speak his words.

"Sir Gavin," he paused. "The Prince you saw on your way to Denrith did also appear to me and commanded that I deliver a message to you this day. He said, 'By the shores of the Crimson River, you shall be made whole.'"

Gavin waited for more, but there was none.

Weston looked at Nias. "He would have to travel through the Forest of Renault to reach the Crimson River."

Nias looked somber. "The message is not mine to change, Weston. I must be on my way."

He mounted his horse and prepared to leave, but first turned to face Gavin.

"You should know, Sir Gavin, that word of your change in allegiance has reached Kifus. The Followers in Chessington tell us that he has sworn to find you and kill you. Contingents of Noble Knights are searching for you as we speak."

Nias looked at Weston, saluted, then turned and galloped back toward Denrith. Gavin and Weston spent a moment in silence as they watched Nias disappear over a grassy knoll in the distance.

Although Gavin had expected such a reaction from Kifus and the Noble Knights eventually, he was not fully prepared to hear Nias's blunt warning, especially since he knew that it was likely very few of the Followers even believed that his heart had truly changed. He felt like an outcast between two kingdoms at war.

"My presence here is putting you and your family in grave danger," Gavin said to Weston.

"I knew the risk when I agreed to bring you to my home. We will be all right."

"I admire your courage, my friend, but I will not be the cause of any more anguish to innocent people." Gavin's gaze left the knoll and rested on Weston. "I know the Noble Knights. They will be ruthless in their search and execution of those abetting a traitor. How do I find the Crimson River?"

"You don't understand, Gavin. The journey there is—" Weston paused.

"What is your concern?" Gavin asked.

"There are regions in the Forest of Renault that are extremely dangerous. Are you familiar with the caralynx?"

"I have heard of such cats, but have never seen one."

"The caralynx of Renault are very aggressive and thus make travel through the forest quite treacherous," Weston said.

"Why are they more dangerous than any other wildcat?" Gavin asked.

"Because of the manner in which they attack. They have skin that joins their forelimbs to their hind limbs. This allows them to glide through the air when leaping from trees, which is where they dwell almost exclusively. They descend silently on their prey from above. What makes them especially dangerous are the dewclaws on their forelimbs."

"Dewclaws?" Gavin said.

"Dewclaws are the usually harmless appendages above the claws on an animal's paws, but the caralynx's dewclaws are highly developed ripping claws. The cats often sharpen this claw on the bark of a black walnut tree, which can poison its prey through an open wound."

"What a lovely creature," Gavin quipped, but Weston did not reply in kind.

"During mating season, they are extremely territorial and aggressive," Weston said.

Gavin shook his head. "I have no choice. I will leave after supper."

Weston looked as though he was going to protest, but remained silent.

That evening during supper, Gavin arrived in the dining

hall dressed and prepared to travel. Weston and his family were all seated at one end of a grand table that had formerly hosted exquisite banquets for many guests. Gavin placed himself in a chair beside Addy.

"I am at a loss for words to express my gratitude for your kindness and gracious hospitality over these past days," Gavin said. "I must, however, take my leave from you."

Addy and Keaton appeared sad and looked down at their plates.

"Where will you go?" Marie asked.

"There is a river that beckons my heart to come," Gavin replied.

"You are hardly fit to ride, my friend, let alone embark on a journey through treacherous country," Weston said, still looking concerned. "I will accompany you."

Gavin smiled at his new friend. "You have given too much already, and this is a journey I must make alone."

"Will you come back to see us?" Addy asked. Keaton looked up with the same question in his eyes.

"You can count on it, little miss," he said, winking at Keaton.

The meal was simple but delicious, as usual. Afterward, Gavin returned to his room to gather his sword and a few miscellaneous items. Addy and Keaton appeared in the doorway.

"We're going to miss you, Sir Gavin," Addy said with big sad eyes. Gavin turned and knelt on one knee. He lifted his good arm, and the two children ran into his embrace. At that moment, Gavin experienced the beginning of the healing of his heart. He held them tight, and some of the ache disappeared.

"I'm going to miss the two of you," he said with tears in his eyes. "I want to thank you for teaching me how to like children."

Addy released her hug, but Keaton held his embrace a little longer. When he finally let go, he turned and ran out of the room. Addy stayed a moment longer. She gently put a hand on Gavin's wounded shoulder.

"When you find Him, will you tell Him hello from Keaton and Adelaide?" Addy asked.

"Find who?" Gavin was somewhat perplexed.

Addy smiled and left the room to find her brother.

Gavin said good-bye to Marie and then walked to the stables, where Weston was saddling Triumph. When all was ready, he turned and looked at Gavin.

"Are you sure you're up for this?" Weston asked. "Couldn't you wait at least until morning? You only have a few hours of daylight left."

"I am compelled, Weston. I have much to sort out. If I am to live at all, I must find my way again."

"I understand."

Gavin mounted Triumph. His sword hung at his side, but there was no whole or skilled arm to use it.

"I put provisions in your pack. You know you are always welcome here," Weston said. Gavin nodded his appreciation.

Weston handed Gavin a long-knife.

"You may find this useful."

Gavin instinctively tried to reach for the knife with his right hand, but his lame arm did not move. He reached across his horse with his left hand and took the knife.

"Thank you," Gavin replied and stowed the knife in his belt.

He looked out across the countryside in all directions.

"The Crimson River flows from the Boundary Mountains across the Brimshire Plains and eventually into the Forest of Renault. Traveling northeast should get you there," Weston said as he pointed. "Be careful, my friend."

Gavin took a deep breath. "Perhaps this time Triumph and I will work together," he said as he patted the steed's powerful neck. Gavin looked down at Weston. "In this short time you have already become as a brother to me."

Gavin extended his left arm to Weston. "That is what the Prince creates between men—brotherhood." Weston grabbed his forearm. "I am honored to have known you, my friend. May the Prince guard and guide you in your quest."

"And you!"

Triumph seemed anxious to be on their way. Gavin crossed the Wickmere River and traveled away from Chessington, on toward a land he had never seen before, searching for a resolution to a forsaken past and a hopeful future.

CHAPTER THIRTEEN

UNDAUNTED QUEST

 Later that evening, Gavin was at the fringes of the Forest of Renault. He made camp and was thankful for the warmth of the season. The sounds of the still night enveloped him. His shoulder was stiff and ached clear to his fingers. He wondered if he would ever be able to use his arm again.

Early the next morning, Gavin broke camp and was quickly underway. He remained alert and cautious as he entered the forest, but hours of peaceful travel eventually calmed his fears. Progress through the forest slowed as the vegetation became dense. At one point, he had to dismount and walk ahead of Triumph just to navigate beneath the sprawling limbs of the trees. After many hours of traveling in this manner, the forest seemed to open slightly. Gavin found a small stream, and he and Triumph drank the cool water to satisfy their thirst. As he went to mount Triumph, the horse became agitated and began to back away from him. Gavin wondered if the horse was reverting to his prior stubborn nature, but then Gavin stopped.

"What is it, boy?" Gavin stroked the horse's neck to soothe him.

Triumph snorted and held his head high while turning it from side to side. The horse then violently turned into Gavin and reared up. The force of the impact sent Gavin reeling to the ground. As he hit, the excruciating pain in his shoulder instantly returned. He was just a couple paces beneath the raised hooves of his powerful stallion, and he wondered if the animal was going to trample him. But then he heard Triumph's scream mix with the spine-chilling screech of a beast from above. Gavin looked up and saw a caralynx gliding toward Triumph with his deadly claws stretched forth to tear into whatever it landed upon. Gavin then understood that had not Triumph turned to meet the attack, the creature would surely have landed on him.

Triumph pounded the air with his hooves. It was too late for the vicious cat to alter its flight enough to avoid the deadly blows. Gavin rolled to the side as the caralynx shrieked again and swiped its deadly dewclaw at Triumph's chest. The cat imbedded the long claw deep into the steed's muscled shoulder, just as a hoof caught the flying predator square in the chest. The hideous sound from the throat of the caralynx was instantly silenced as the tremendous force of Triumph's kick sent the creature flying four paces in the opposite direction, simultaneously tearing muscle and hide from the steed's shoulder.

Gavin rose to a kneeling position and pulled the long-knife from his belt as the cat hit the ground and recovered. Triumph whinnied in pain and turned away from the wildcat. The enraged caralynx instantly poised itself to pounce on the retreating horse. It sprang again with all its claws extended. Gavin was just to the side of Triumph and leapt at the creature to meet it in the air. He sunk the long-knife deep into the side of the animal. It shrieked, turned midair to attempt a swipe at Gavin, and bumped harmlessly against the body of Triumph. It fell to the ground, and Gavin quickly pulled his sword from the scabbard, but there was no need. The caralynx made a weak attempt to rise, then sunk lifelessly to the ground.

Triumph circled and whinnied in pain, and Gavin went to his horse and grabbed the reins.

"Easy, boy…easy," Gavin tried to calm the animal so he could inspect the injury. Triumph settled, and Gavin could see that the claw had sunk deep but had not penetrated beyond the powerful shoulder muscles. The wound was bleeding profusely, however. He doused a cloth in the stream and carefully began to wash the wound. Triumph's pain was obvious, and Gavin paused. He stroked the horse's face and neck.

"Triumph, you are indeed a magnificent horse… I was never worthy of such a gallant stallion as you."

Gavin continued to clean the wound but became worried that the caralynx's dewclaw might have contained poison—only time would tell. Gavin decided to press onward since he had already traveled deep into the forest and there was as much trek behind him as there was ahead. He walked beside Triumph, and within an hour it was clear that the stallion was beginning to suffer from the effects of something more than just a gash. Triumph's head lowered and he began to stumble. Gavin stopped and made his horse lie down on the forest floor. He washed the wound again.

Sadness began to overwhelm him, for he knew there was nothing he could do to save the life of his faithful steed.

"I am sorry, old friend. You took the strike of that wildcat for me, and now I can do nothing for you."

Gavin knelt beside him and laid his hand on the animal's neck. Triumph nickered as if to say, "It's all right, master… That is what I do."

Gavin could not help the tears that welled up in his eyes as he remembered the many times Triumph had carried him victoriously into and out of battle. The hours passed, and Gavin did not leave Triumph. The animal's breathing became shallow and weak, and Gavin knew its end was near.

Before long, Gavin heard the approach of a beast through the wall of trees behind him. There was no stealth in the approach, and he quickly realized that it was not just one but many that were coming upon him. His heart began to race, and he drew his sword, holding it as best he could with his left hand. The jagged form of mounted men slowly became discernable as they approached, but Gavin's fear only increased, for he had been in this situation once before.

He clenched his hand into a fist and wondered if the evil brutes who had wounded him were coming to finish the job they had started many weeks earlier. Their forms were large and menacing, and Gavin considered fleeing, but they had already seen him, and it would now be futile. Gavin stood as five massive warriors atop their warhorses broke through the trees and approached him. They were equal in stature to the brutes who had nearly killed him, but Gavin sensed a different air about them. Even still, he could not deny the fear that swelled within his bosom.

They too formed a semicircle around Gavin. The leader dismounted before him. He stood a full head taller. He looked sternly at Gavin and then to Triumph lying at Gavin's feet. The man knelt down and placed a hand on Triumph's shoulder near the wound of the caralynx. He turned and looked at his companions.

"It is a Kasian," the man said in a deep voice. He rose and faced Gavin. "You are Gavin of Chessington?"

"I am."

"You are fortunate to have made it this far alone," he said.

Gavin looked down at Triumph. "The caralynx would have killed me were it not for Triumph."

"It is not the caralynx I am referring to," he said bluntly. "The Dark Knight desires your blood, for his warriors have foolishly underestimated the power of the Prince and His plans." The warrior quickly scanned the surrounding area.

"I don't understand," Gavin replied. "Who are you?"

The warrior looked at Gavin and clenched his jaw.

"I was your enemy and am now commanded to be your guide," he responded.

Gavin sensed the reticence in the man, and he understood that his past was as difficult for a messenger of the Prince to overcome as it was for himself. Gavin lowered his eyes and saw the mark of the Prince on the pommel of the warrior's sword.

"I doubt, sir, that either of us should understand the ways of the Prince in regard to my life. What is your way with me?" Gavin asked, eager to be done with this conversation, for the pain in his heart was quickly rising again. He sheathed his sword.

The warrior hesitated and then turned to his men.

"Brock, dismount. He will need your horse to ride. Trustan,

stay with Brock until we return. You know what to do, so be quick about it and stay alert!"

One of the warriors dismounted and held the reins out to Gavin. Gavin knelt down to Triumph and stroked his neck. He thought perhaps the horse was already gone.

"Good-bye, my friend." He knew that he would never see his faithful equine companion again, and his heart grieved. He found it difficult to leave his dying horse, but the warriors seemed impatient. He slowly stood and took the reins of the warrior's horse.

Once Gavin mounted, the leader wasted no time in getting underway as Gavin and the three warriors continued on toward the far side of the Forest of Renault. They traveled for two full days, navigating the forest landscape. There were no more encounters with caralynx, and Gavin deduced that their numbers were too great for any wildcat to threaten them. Still, they proceeded with great caution, often stopping to listen and even changing directions for a time. Gavin learned that the leader's name was Lindan, but unless Gavin initiated it, there was very little conversation other than that required to fulfill the journey. Gavin did not mind. One of the other warriors was as cool toward him as Lindan, but the one named Porunth warmed slightly. Gavin found him a fairly amicable fellow with bright red hair and a full beard to match.

During the second evening's camp, Gavin sat down beside Porunth. After an exchange of some idle pleasantries, he felt he could approach the man with some questions that had plagued his mind for many days.

"Porunth, I have encountered many knights and warriors from throughout the kingdom, but never have I seen warriors such as you. I can only assume that you must be Silent Warriors."

"You have not seen us, but we have seen you…many times." Porunth smiled. "Our home is with the King across the Great Sea, but our mission now lies in Arrethtrae, ever since the revolt."

"Lucius?" Gavin asked.

"Yes. He and his Shadow Warriors have brought chaos to the kingdom, but the Prince will prevail."

"I believe I have experienced some of the chaos firsthand." Gavin massaged his right arm as he spoke.

Porunth's friendly countenance became serious. "The Shadow Warriors are cold-blooded and ruthless," he said, and Gavin sensed a life of memories girding up his solemn response. He looked at Gavin. "You are extremely fortunate to have survived that encounter. I must tell you we have heard that Lucius and the Shadow Warriors have made you a priority target."

Porunth nodded in Lindan's direction and lowered his voice. "That is why Commander Lindan is so concerned. The quicker we are rid of you, the better he will feel. And you have to remember that the Silent Warriors watched you torment the Followers of the Prince for a very long time, much to the hindrance of our own work for the King. You are not necessarily a, shall we say, favored ally. The ways of the Prince are often a mystery to us."

This helped Gavin understand Lindan's demeanor, but he needed a moment to assimilate the information that Porunth had just shared.

"Why would Lucius be so concerned with me?" he asked.

"Because the Prince is concerned with you. Lucius is reacting as an enemy should—destroy that which an adversary seeks," Porunth replied.

Gavin shook his head in confusion.

"The Noble Knights think they are serving the King and want to kill me. Lucius and the Shadow Warriors hate the King and want to kill me. The Followers of the Prince don't trust me, and the Silent Warriors nearly despise me. I feel as though the whole kingdom is pursuing me and desires my destruction. Is there anyone who doesn't want me dead or think me a villain?"

"There is One," Porunth said as he moved toward his bedroll.

"May I ask you one more question, Porunth?" Gavin said quietly.

Porunth nodded.

"Lindan said my horse was a Kasian. What did he mean by that?" he asked.

"A Kasian is a breed of horse that comes from only one place: the Kingdom Across the Sea. Only the King's court and His Silent Warriors are allowed to own them. To see one in Arrethtrae that does not belong to a Silent Warrior is strange indeed. It is a mystery to us as to why the King would allow the charge of one to an Arrethtraen such as you."

"It is as much a mystery to me, sir," Gavin replied.

"It is how we found you," Porunth said.

"How so?"

"The Kasians hear things in a unique way. I suppose much

like a bat that flies in the dark. The night and the fog are not a hindrance to them," Porunth said.

"How did that help you find me in the depths of this forest?" Gavin asked.

Porunth paused. "A Kasian can hear the death of one of its kind."

Gavin thought of Triumph and was deeply saddened.

"We are not allowed to leave the carcass of a Kasian behind. It is divided and removed or burned or buried. Brock and Trustan have taken care of it. I am sorry, Gavin. Your loss is great, for a Kasian is more loyal than a mastiff hound," he said.

The evidence of Gavin's foolishness and ignorance enveloped him in every aspect of his life: the fallacy of the order of the Noble Knights to which he had dedicated his life, the persecution first of the Prince and then His Followers, and now even his lack of understanding as to the significance of his loyal steed. He had lost it all and wondered at the purpose of his appointment at the Crimson River. Was he riding toward judgment and condemnation or pardon and acquittal? He didn't even know who, if anyone, would be there. His apprehension mounted, and sleep was elusive.

On the third day, the far edge of the forest opened to the country and the trees gave way to lush, grassy hills. The Crimson River lazily wound its way across the vibrant country before entering the Forest of Renault. Gavin could hear the faint bubbling of water over the mossy rocks in the distance, but here the river widened and the water was still and mirrored the sky and opposite shoreline perfectly. Lindan halted his men at the tree line and scanned the area.

"Dismount," Lindan commanded Gavin.

Gavin complied. Lindan pointed to the reins of Gavin's mount and held out his hand. Gavin handed him the reins.

"What now?" Gavin asked.

Lindan pointed and Gavin looked in that direction. Beside the Crimson River, beneath a sprawling shade tree, Gavin saw the form of a gallant knight that could belong to only one man. Gavin's heart quickened, for he had fearfully hoped that he might see the Prince again.

Gavin turned to Lindan. "Is He here to rule the kingdom?"

"No, He is here for you," Lindan replied. "When He comes again to Arrethtrae, it will be not as a pauper but as a king, and every soul in the kingdom will know that it is He who reigns!"

Gavin looked again toward the figure at the river. "What does He want of me?"

But there was no reply. Lindan had already turned his men back toward the forest.

Gavin ran at first, and as the distance diminished, the emblem on the Prince's shield left no doubt as to His identity. Gavin slowed and approached cautiously, not sure how to respond. With each step he became increasingly confused by his emotions. He was overcome by the dichotomy of his life. He was grieved by his actions, yet joyful for a second chance. Here before him stood the One who brought the forces of the kingdom into submission and caused the hands of evil men to tremble. The last few steps became cumbersome, and Gavin was beset by the deeds of his former life against One so royal. Gavin approached the Prince, fell at His feet, and wept.

"Stand up, Sir Gavin," the Prince said.

"No, my Lord, for I am too ashamed to take in Your gaze. I cannot bear the grief that I have caused You, the King, and Your people. I cannot right the wrongs nor repay the debt I owe You. I am not worthy to stand before You, my Lord!"

The Prince knelt down and gently placed His hands on either side of Gavin's head. "You are right, Gavin, you cannot repay your debt, but you can be forgiven. And this I offer you, for I see your broken heart. Look upon Me and accept My forgiveness, for I am a Prince of the future and not the past."

Gavin slowly lifted his head and looked into the eyes of fire that burned with compassion, not condemnation.

"Let go of your past, and look to Mine, where I died for you. Yield to Me, and I will make you a true Knight of the Prince."

The Prince grabbed Gavin's left hand with His own and slowly lifted him up. Gavin remembered his crusade to rid the kingdom of the Prince and His Followers and wished them to be the echoes of a bad dream, but the images and emotions were too real. As he took in the powerful gaze of the Prince, he saw a future that could shatter his past and restore in him the heart of a nobleman. Gavin was a passionate man, and his passion for truth had been turned inside out and shaken. Here, near the still waters of the Crimson River, Gavin accepted the forgiveness of the Prince and embraced the hope of a restored future…his future. He laid his head on the Prince's chest and felt the embrace of the King's Son around his shoulders.

"My Prince, my heart aches to serve You, and yet I am not able to even lift my sword. How can I become a Knight of the Prince and be of any service to You, my Lord?" Gavin asked. The skill and ability of his former life had abandoned him, and now he had nothing to offer the One whom he had persecuted.

"I do not need the strength of your arm to make a knight of you, Gavin. All I need is your heart, and that you have given," the Prince replied.

Gavin found peace in the words of the Prince—true, lasting peace. His search was over, and already he sensed the beginning of a new quest.

The Prince tarried long with Gavin and explained many things. He taught him the true and intimate meaning of the Code in such a way that Gavin felt as though he were hearing it for the first time. The words on the ancient parchment lifted from the page and meshed with his mind and heart as the Prince imparted great wisdom and knowledge to him. They talked of things past, things present, and things future. With new understanding, his passion for the King and the Code welled up within him once again as the Prince opened his eyes to a new vision for the kingdom of Arrethtrae.

As the days passed, Gavin's wonder and awe at the wisdom and the character of the King's Son continued to grow. He discovered new strength and purpose in His presence. All of the kingdom seemed to make sense now. He pitied the Noble Knights he had left behind, for their eyes were blind and this new truth was invigorating. He thought how ironic it was that those chosen and trained to prepare the way for the Prince were so blind that they not only did not recognize Him, but they were the instruments of His death. He wanted to shout the truth of the Prince from every street corner in Chessington.

"I understand the Code like never before, my Prince," Gavin said after one of their many discourses on the King and His plan for Arrethtrae. "I am anxious to share Your truth with all of the people of Chessington."

The Prince smiled. "Gavin, your heart is now set upon the right course, but you are not ready."

Gavin's enthusiasm faded. "What do I lack, my Lord?"

"You lack a sword."

Gavin's heart became heavy. He looked down at his lame arm and knew that he would never be able to wield a sword with it again, for as the days had passed, no strength returned.

"I will go as a knight without a sword to move the hearts of men to You, my Lord. I am not afraid," Gavin said.

"You may indeed reach the ears of men with your words, but you must remember that your enemy is neither the men of dissension nor even the Noble Knights, but the forces of the Dark Knight and his Shadow Warriors. They would run you through before a word could pass your lips."

Sorrow filled Gavin's heart as he realized the truth of the Prince's words. A moment of illumination filled his mind.

"You were dead and yet now live… Surely there is a way to heal my arm," he said with new hope.

"No, Gavin, your weakness will be My strength, and I will sustain you," the Prince replied. "Not even the forces of the Dark Knight will prevail against you!"

"How is this possible, my Prince?"

The Prince stood. "Rise up and draw your sword."

Gavin stood and drew his sword with his left hand. He looked upon it and realized once again that this was the sword that had brought great affliction to the Followers of the Prince. The Prince held out His hand, and Gavin yielded his sword to Him. He brought the pommel of the sword to His lips and kissed the seal of the King. He returned the sword to Gavin, and somehow it felt different.

"The sword is the same, but your mind is enlightened, and therefore the sword's purpose is now magnanimous," the Prince said. "You have one good arm. I will train you so your skill in its use will surpass even your previous ability."

Gavin hesitated. He did not believe he could even get beyond the awkward feeling of holding the sword in his left hand. "Your confidence in me is unmerited, my Lord, but I will try."

And the training began.

For many days, Gavin struggled and became frustrated, for it was difficult to feel so inept with a weapon that had once felt like an extension of his body. However, once it became natural to hold, progress transpired rapidly, for the knowledge of mastery was already available to him. Each day the melodic clink of steel filled the country air, and the pain of his past receded beyond memory. At first the steely rhythm was slow and broken, but as the dawn of each day came, the audible intensity of the exchanges was a clear indication of Gavin's improvement. The Prince was patient and tireless as He honed Gavin's skills to perfection. Neither the sun, nor the rain, nor the wind of the day deterred their sessions, and Gavin began to feel whole once again. The persona of a true and gallant knight filled his soul. By the end of the training, Gavin's mastery exceeded far beyond his prior level, and there was not a blade in all of Arrethtrae that could compare.

One morning after Gavin had eaten, he arose and came to the Prince to begin their session, but the Prince did not draw His sword.

Gavin tilted his head slightly. "What is it, my Lord?"

"Your training is nearly complete. Soon you must leave Me to fulfill your mission, and I must return to My Father."

"I will not rest until every man, woman, and child in Chessington is granted the opportunity to hear and believe in You, my Lord," Gavin said.

The Prince shook his head. "No, Gavin. I do not send you to Chessington. I send you to the far reaches of the kingdom."

Once again, Gavin was bewildered at the ways of the Prince. He wrestled with his former biases regarding the people of the kingdom—Outdwellers, many of whom were sworn enemies of Chessington.

"But the people of Chessington are Your people, my Prince. The Outdwellers are at enmity against Chessington and are not worthy," Gavin replied.

"All people in the Kingdom of Arrethtrae belong to the King. None are worthy and few will find the way, but all are called. The King's people of Chessington have hardened their hearts toward Me. Because of this you will make knights of all people in all regions, and Chessington must suffer many trials. This is the age of the Outdwellers."

In spite of all he had learned from the Prince, Gavin was again perplexed. As he slowly discarded the residue of his own wisdom, he became awestruck at the depth and width and height of the wisdom of the Prince. One city was far too small to contain the compassion of the King and His Son, and an excitement began to build within Gavin as he understood the magnitude of his new mission.

"Forgive me, my Prince… I understand."

The Prince looked into Gavin's eyes, and Gavin felt once again as though his heart were being examined.

"You must beware of the Dark Knight and his Shadow Warriors, for they lie in wait to kill you. Are you prepared for the great adversity that will come if you serve Me?" the Prince asked.

"I am, my Prince!"

"Then kneel."

Gavin knelt, and the Prince drew His sword.

"You have knelt as Gavin of Chessington. By the might of

the King and the power of His sword, I knight you Sir Gavinaugh of Arrethtrae, Knight of the Prince!"

There at the shores of the Crimson River, the Prince knighted a young man and finished the transformation from enemy to servant.

"Rise, Sir Gavinaugh. I have made all things new in you. Your name, your sword, and your mission will be the witness of your belief in Me to all people."

Gavinaugh rose, and there was a fire in his heart that burned hotter than ever before, for now it was fueled by the inexhaustible truth of the Prince.

The Prince placed a hand on Gavinaugh's chest. "Go forth, Sir Gavinaugh, and make the Kingdom of Arrethtrae into one land, one people, and one knightly order. Take My freedom to them and the promise of My return. Your quest is noble and you are worthy to fulfill it!"

Gavinaugh placed his hand over the Prince's to make his oath. "To the last beat of my heart, I will, my Prince. I so swear!"

CHESSINGTON'S HOPE

 The tale of Sir Gavinaugh is one that has reverberated in the great halls of castles throughout the kingdom, for his quest to journey to the ends of the kingdom is renowned, and his fierce battles against the Noble Knights and the Shadow Warriors are the fabric of legends. Unfortunately, I, Cedric of Chessington, must pause just now to ready my steed and my weapons for battle. Our ranks are set and the orders are soon to come, for the Prince is drawing near. What a day this will be! The great city below us is in peril, and her citizens do tremble in fear, for they know that the Dark Knight and his evil army come for them. For many years they turned their hearts away from the Prince and the truth He brought, but now they understand and their deliverance is at hand. I pity them for their fear and rejoice for them in their hope. The Prince is here!

Perhaps very soon you will join me again to finish the

glorious tale of the gallant Sir Gavinaugh and his quest for the kingdom of Arrethtrae. It is a tale of adventure, love, adversity, and great struggle—a tale that compels me to tell it, for the legacy gives purpose to this battle ahead! Until then…Godspeed, my friend!

DISCUSSION QUESTIONS

To further facilitate the understanding of the biblical allegory of this series, a few discussion questions and answers are provided below.

CHAPTER 1
1. What group of people do the Noble Knights represent?
2. Who does Kifus represent?
3. Kifus lives at the remnants of Lord Quinn's palace. This is also the place where the Noble Knights have their discussions and training. What is this representative of?
4. In this palace is a special room: the Chamber of the Code. Only Lord Kifus and the top five Noble Knights are given access to this room. The people of Chessington aren't ever allowed into this chamber. What does this symbolize?

CHAPTER 2
1. What biblical event does the "incident" in this chapter represent?

CHAPTER 3
1. Who do you think Demus might represent? Why?

CHAPTER 4

1. What biblical encounters are represented when Demus, Braden, and Jayden attack the stranger in the first part of this chapter? Does this event seem familiar? Find an example of this event in the Bible.

2. Do you remember in this chapter as well as in *Kingdom's Edge* when Demus asks the stranger if he really is the King's Son? Find the Scripture verses that this question alludes to.

3. When Kifus announces his conviction that the stranger is from the domain of the Dark Knight, what does this represent?

4. At one point during the Noble Knights' discussion, Demus leaves, saying he doesn't consent to the direction the discussion is going. What might this represent?

5. Once the Noble Knights decide to capture the stranger, Kifus says the way won't be too difficult because one of the Followers "has a fancy for silver." Who does this Follower represent biblically?

6. At the end of the chapter, Demus and Gavin discuss the stranger one last time. Demus says, "Instead of taking my life, he spared it. We went to kill him, and yet he showed us mercy." What is this a foreshadowing of, and what does it symbolize?

CHAPTER 5

1. Gavin thinks the stranger looks defeated, like a "helpless lamb" during the interrogation by the Noble

Knights. What does this symbolize? Find a verse to support your answer.

2. The stranger's physical abuse by Bremrick during his interrogation is an allegory of what?

3. Kifus finally asks the stranger if he is the Son of the King, and the stranger replies, "I AM." What event does this represent?

CHAPTER 6

1. Immediately after the death of the stranger, Gavin assumes that Chessington's problems are over because he doesn't think anyone would continue to follow a dead leader. How is Gavin right, and how is he wrong?

2. What important biblical event is symbolized by the doors of the Chamber of the Code being destroyed? Why is this so important?

CHAPTER 7

1. In this chapter we hear that the Followers stole the body of their leader, whom they claimed was the Prince. Do you remember from *Kingdom's Edge* what really happened? What biblical event does this portray?

2. Up until this point, we've been getting another perspective on events that occurred in *Kingdom's Edge*. However, the death of Severin is a new incident: what biblical event does it portray?

3. Read Severin's speech to the people again. Then read Stephen's final speech in Acts 7:2–53. Does it surprise

you that a common Jew could be so knowledgeable about Jewish history and theory? Why do you think this is?

4. After the death of Severin, we are given the most obvious clue yet on Gavin's biblical character. Who does he represent?

CHAPTER 8

1. Gavin and Kifus are disgusted to learn that the Followers call themselves Knights of the Prince. What might this represent?

2. Gavin is full of zeal to eliminate the Followers, so Kifus issues an edict for Gavin to seek out and arrest the Followers. What does this portray?

3. Despite his abuse, William shares words of compassion about the Prince and His ways with his captors. Can you find a verse in the Bible that supports William's attitude? When William tells Gavin that the Followers have dispersed, what does that represent?

CHAPTER 9

1. Who might the swordsmith represent?

2. After Gavin meets massive warriors chasing a peasant girl, he realizes he was mistaken in disregarding their existence. This was because he was "too intelligent" to believe the stories about them. Too many people intellectualize Christianity and claim that religion without

proof is false. This teaching discredits the concept of faith. What does the Bible say about faith?

3. Gavin remarks, "The affairs of Outdwellers are not the affairs of the Noble Knights." What does this attitude represent?

CHAPTER 10

1. In light of everything that happens in this chapter, what do you think Denrith represents?

2. When Gavin is near death, he realizes that although he lived his life in a way he thought honored the King, he was empty in the end. Why?

3. In this chapter, Gavin receives a unique opportunity: he is given a front-row seat to the spiritual battle for his own soul. Find a verse in the Bible that talks about this.

4. Read the account of Paul's conversion in Acts 9:3–8. Look at verse 5 in light of what the Prince says to Gavin. What do you think it means?

CHAPTER 11

1. Weston places incredible faith in Gavin because he believes "in the Prince and in His power to transform the hearts of men." In turn, Bensen, although suspicious of Gavin, risks his life because of his trust in Weston. Have you ever placed your faith in someone solely because of Jesus' transforming power? What happened?

2. What does Gavin's flight through Eagle Pass represent?

CHAPTER 12

1. When Gavin talks to Addy and Keaton about the Prince, he says, "That which I thought was right is wrong. And that which I thought was wrong is true." Have you ever found out that something you believed was not as it seemed? What might have helped you make a better decision? Find a Bible verse that talks about good and evil.

2. Addy says the Prince did more wonderful things than could be contained in "all the parchment in the kingdom." What Bible verse in John 21 is this alluding to?

3. When Gavin finally eats, he is famished. Find a verse in the Bible that also talks about Saul being hungry after three days of blindness and hunger.

4. After he drops his sword, Gavin reflects, "With this sword I wrought devastation when I believed I was bringing justice—for the King, no less!" What does this represent?

5. When Gavin explains how he acquired Triumph, he says the horse was a gift from a man "on his way to a distant land." The next day this stranger gave Triumph to Gavin's mother and said, "The compassion of One heals many sorrows." Who was this man, and what did he mean by his words?

6. Weston is pleased by Gavin's state of heart, which he says is necessary to follow the Prince. What is this attitude, and why is it so important?

7. Gavin almost dies from a severe fever caused by his

wound from the Shadow Warriors. His life is spared when Sir Nias brings a healing salve to apply to Gavin's wound. What does this event portray?

8. What do you think is significant about the name of the river Gavin must travel to?

9. Kifus and the Noble Knights are enraged that Gavin has become a Follower, and they've sworn to hunt down and execute him. Find a verse in Acts that shows the allegory.

10. Gavin is amazed to find how quickly Weston becomes like a brother to him, and Weston replies that the Prince creates brotherhood between men. Find some verses in the Bible that talk about this.

CHAPTER 13

1. Lindan, the head Silent Warrior who escorts Gavin, says that the Dark Knight wants Gavin dead because he underestimated the Prince's plans. What does this mean?

2. Another Silent Warrior, Porunth, remarks, "The ways of the Prince are often a mystery to us." Find a Bible verse that supports this view.

3. Porunth also tells Gavin that there is one person who doesn't want Gavin dead or think harshly of him. Who is this person?

4. Gavin asks Lindan if the Prince has come back to rule Arrethtrae, but Lindan says that when the Prince does come back, "it will be not as a pauper but as a king, and every soul in the kingdom will know that it is He

who reigns!" What is Lindan referring to? Which biblical event does this symbolize? Find a verse in Philippians that supports your answer.

5. The Prince tells Gavin that he cannot repay his debt, but he can be forgiven because of his broken heart. Find some verses in the Bible that address "broken hearts."

6. The Prince also says He doesn't need Gavin's strength, but his heart. Find a verse in the Bible that talks about this. Also find a verse that talks about the true peace Gavin experienced.

7. Gavin journeys to the Crimson River to gain new understanding about the Code and the ways of the Prince from the Prince Himself. Why do you think this is important? Read Galatians 1:15–18 to help find your answer.

8. In this chapter, it says "the Prince opened [Gavin's] eyes," and Gavin "pitied the Noble Knights he had left behind, for their eyes were blind." What does this symbolize? Find some Bible verses that address spiritual blindness.

9. What is the significance of Gavin's weakened right arm, and what does this represent? Find a passage in 2 Corinthians to support your answer.

10. What is the significance of the Prince's statement, "The sword is the same, but your mind is enlightened, and therefore the sword's purpose is now magnanimous"? What about "It was difficult [for Gavin] to

feel so inept with a weapon that had once felt like an extension of his body"?

11. What is the allegorical meaning behind the King and the Prince's love for the entire kingdom? Find a verse to support your answer.

12. What biblical event is allegorized by Gavin's name change? Find the first instance where Saul's new name is used in the Bible. Then find a verse that talks about things made new.

ANSWERS TO
DISCUSSION QUESTIONS

CHAPTER 1

1. The religious leaders of Israel during the time of Jesus.
2. Caiaphas, the high priest at the time of Jesus Christ's death.
3. The remnants of King Solomon's temple.
4. In the Old Testament, the Ten Commandments were kept in the ark of the covenant, and only the high priests were allowed to be in the Holy of Holies, where the ark was kept. This was because the common Jews needed an intercessor (the priests) to speak to God and offer sacrifices asking God to forgive them for their sins. Although the ark of the covenant had been hidden, or lost, or destroyed by the time of Jesus and was not in the Holy of Holies, the Chamber of the Code was used to depict this sacred room.

CHAPTER 2

1. The woman caught in adultery, who Jesus prevented from being stoned.

CHAPTER 3

1. Demus represents Nicodemus, the Pharisee who came to ask Jesus questions about how to be saved.

CHAPTER 4

1. This represents the many times the Pharisees attempted to catch Jesus making a mistake or teaching the people false doctrine. Read Mark 12:13–34, and note the three men who spoke with Jesus and tried to lure Him into speaking against the Scriptures.

2. Nicodemus came to speak with Jesus by night. Their discussion is in John 3:1–21. Nicodemus also defended Jesus during a discussion among the Pharisees (John 7:40–53).

3. When the Pharisees accuse Jesus of being in league with Beelzebub, or Satan (Matthew 12:24).

4. Joseph of Arimathea, a prominent and powerful Jew, had no part in the capture and crucifixion of Jesus (Luke 23:50–51).

5. Judas Iscariot, the traitor (Matthew 26:14–16).

6. That the stranger would actually die for him. This symbolizes Jesus Christ's death on the cross for us.

CHAPTER 5

1. Jesus' silence during His trial, which was prophesized in Isaiah 53:7.

2. Jesus is struck during His trial (see John 18:22).

3. When the high priest questions Jesus about His identity and Jesus replies that He is the Son of God (Luke 22:66–71).

CHAPTER 6

1. Gavin is wrong in thinking that their problems are over, but he's correct that the people of Chessington would not follow a dead leader. However, they would follow a living one!

2. The tearing of the veil of the temple (Mark 15:38). The tearing of the veil was significant because it symbolized that everyone had access to God themselves. Jesus had become the mediator for all people, common or noble (see Hebrews 8:11; 9).

CHAPTER 7

1. The "decaying dead leader" of the Followers was the living, breathing Prince. This event allegorizes the Resurrection of Jesus Christ.

2. The stoning of Stephen, the first martyr (Acts 6:8–7:60).

3. The Holy Spirit gives wisdom and knowledge to His people. He also gives peace—even in death, Severin and Stephen were peaceful men. Isn't it amazing Stephen's last act was to request that the men who killed them not be charged by God for their actions?

4. Saul (Acts 7:58).

CHAPTER 8

1. The Followers include the name of the Prince in their own name, Knights of the Prince, just as Jesus Christ's followers came to be called Christians.

2. This represents the high priest giving Saul letters authorizing him to bind any believers he caught and bring them to Jerusalem (Acts 9:1–2). It marks the beginning of Saul's persecution of the church. Read Galatians 1:13–14 and Acts 8:1–3.

3. Matthew 5:44: "But I say to you, love your enemies, bless those who curse you, do good to those who hate you, and pray for those who spitefully use you and persecute you." (See the full passage in Matthew 5:43–48.) This represents when the Christians fled after Stephen's murder (Acts 8:4).

CHAPTER 9

1. A Christian who is a preacher or teacher to others. Read Acts 4:5–14 for an example of disciples who were "troublemakers" because of their knowledge of the Bible.

2. The Bible has quite a bit to say about faith. For example, Matthew 17:20 states, "For assuredly, I say to you, if you have faith as a mustard seed, you will say to this mountain, 'Move from here to there,' and it will move; and nothing will be impossible for you." Another verse says, "Then Jesus called a little child to Him, set him in the midst of them, and said, 'Assuredly, I say to you, unless you are converted and become as little children, you will by no means enter the kingdom of heaven" (Matthew 18:2–3). Faith is essential to serve Christ.

3. The common Jewish perspective at that time that all Gentiles (non-Jews) were unworthy of God's attention or help. Read the story of Jesus and the Woman at the Well in John 4:4–26 (focus on verse 9).

CHAPTER 10

1. Damascus.
2. He wasn't living for the Prince. This represents that true purpose in life comes from a Christ-centered life.
3. Ephesians 6:12.
4. Acts 9:5: "It is hard for you to kick against the goads." Paul was finding no peace because he was battling against God's plan for his life. Biblically, Paul's conversion was an exchange between Jesus and Paul only. The allegory depicts the Shadow Warriors to show that if Paul had not chosen to follow Jesus, he would have continued to be a tool of Satan and would have died an unsaved man.

CHAPTER 11

1. Answer based on personal experience.
2. The disciples helping Saul flee from pursuing Jews by lowering him in a basket over the wall at Damascus (Acts 9:23–25).

CHAPTER 12

1. Answer based on personal experience; Isaiah 5:20.
2. John 21:25.

3. Acts 9:9, 19.

4. The Pharisees became experts on the Law, which was God's Word. However, they used the Law without grace or mercy to elevate themselves, which Jesus called hypocrisy.

5. This man from a distant land was a Silent Warrior. He was referring to the point in time when the Prince would give up His own life for the kingdom because of His compassion. This refers to Jesus Christ's crucifixion and restoration for the world.

6. Gavin was beginning to be truly humble. This is important in our lives as well, because humility is necessary to receive God's forgiveness (Matthew 23:12).

7. Ananias's visit to Saul to heal him from his blindness. Read Acts 9:10–18.

8. The Crimson River represents the crimson blood of Jesus Christ that cleanses us from our sins.

9. Acts 9:23.

10. Matthew 12:50.

CHAPTER 13

1. The King was using Gavin to do His work even before he was a Knight of the Prince, much to the anger of the Dark Knight. This is allegorical to the fact that God used Paul even before he was a Christian. Although Paul's intentions were for evil, God used them for good. Paul persecuted the Christians so severely that they were forced to leave Jerusalem,

thereby spreading the gospel of Jesus Christ across the land, even to the Gentiles.

2. Isaiah 55:8–9 and 1 Peter 1:12.

3. The Prince.

4. The return of the Prince to rule and to reign; this represents the second coming of Jesus Christ (Philippians 2:10–11).

5. Psalm 34:18 and 147:3.

6. Heart (Psalm 147:10–11) and peace (Philippians 4:7).

7. Paul says he did not confer with flesh and blood to understand his new relationship with Jesus Christ. We should be careful and consult God's Holy Word as the source of truth in our relationship with Him as well.

8. It symbolizes when the Holy Spirit comes to dwell in us and gives us wisdom and understanding about things we may have always seen but never truly understood (Psalm 146:8; Isaiah 29:18; and Isaiah 42:7).

9. Paul's thorn in the flesh (2 Corinthians 12:7–10). God allowed a messenger of Satan to give Paul this thorn to keep him humble, just as Gavinaugh received his wound from Devinoux, a warrior of the Dark Knight.

10. Paul had to learn how to use the Word of God *for* God with the perspective of Jesus being the Messiah as foretold in the Old Testament, and it was probably different to think in that way. Having been very knowledgeable on Old Testament Law, doctrine, and prophecy, Paul had to apply this knowledge in a whole new way.

11. God's love for all people, not just the Jews (John 3:16).
12. When Saul's name is changed to Paul (Acts 13:9; 2 Corinthians 5:17).

The River

Written for Kingdom's Call

Music and Lyrics by Emily Elizabeth Black
Edited by Brittney Dyanne Black

1. There's a ri - ver far from here
2. I remem - ber when I first heard His voice
3. I hear His voice to-day calling loud and clear

148

149

AUTHOR'S COMMENTARY

The conversion of Paul is undeniably a spectacular example of Jesus Christ's dramatic intervention in the life of one man. The story itself is a faith-building testimony, for by the world's standards, Paul had everything to lose and nothing to gain. He was a man of power, wealth, influence, and comfort, but once he became a Christian, he was hunted, outcast, poor, and persecuted. A naysayer might claim that Paul was only looking for fame, but promoting the theological views of someone else is a strange way to gain fame. What is remarkable about Paul is that he carried his zeal to persecute the followers of Jesus over to his efforts to preach and promote Christ to the world. There apparently was never a time of apathy in his life. His impact on the world for the gospel of Christ is second only to Jesus Himself.

The character of Gavinaugh was difficult to portray in *Kingdom's Call* simply because he is first an enemy and persecutor of the Prince before he becomes a champion for His cause. It is therefore challenging to allow too much sympathy for our hero until his "road to Damascus" encounter. In *Kingdom's Quest,* the compassion and courage of Sir Gavinaugh make him an endearing character that the reader is easily able to identify with.

I have endeavored to capture portions of Paul's spiritual life in allegorical form. The events that chronicle his life are so fascinating and adventuresome by themselves that I find my writing grossly inadequate by comparison. I hope this book will open your eyes to the spiritual battle that was raging as a result of God's profoundly earthshaking design to establish His church in this fallen, dark world. Above all, my prayer is that you will search God's Holy Word and discover the adventure He has waiting for you!

> *Therefore, if anyone is in Christ, he is a new*
> *creation; old things have passed away;*
> *behold, all things have become new.*
> —2 CORINTHIANS 5:17